Case of the
Fugitive Firebug

by SCOTT CORBETT

Illustrated by Paul Frame

SCHOLASTIC BOOK SERVICES
NEW YORK • TORONTO • LONDON • AUCKLAND • SYDNEY

Books by Scott Corbett available through
Scholastic Book Services:
> The Case of the Fugitive Firebug
> The Lemonade Trick

Copyright © 1969 by Scott Corbett. This edition is published
by Scholastic Book Services, a division of Scholastic Magazines,
Inc., by arrangement with Little, Brown and Company, Inc. in
association with the Atlantic Monthly Press.

1st printing . . . . September 1970

Printed in the U.S.A.

To My Mother with Love

1

STANDING IN THE MOONLIGHT, Inspector Tearle gazed out at his office. It was twenty feet from his second floor bedroom window, and gave him a certain distinction. He was probably the only detective in the world who had his office in a tree.

During the winter Roger Tearle's room had to do double duty as bedroom and office, but all summer he used the tree house that he and his sister Shirley and Thumbs Thorndyke had built in the big oak in the back yard. Inside the tree house, behind the pieces of tarpaulin that covered the windows and doorway for the night, were a desk, a chair, a two-drawer steel filing cabinet, and a telephone that connected with a receiver in the kitchen.

At the moment he was contemplating his office with unusual pride. Perhaps somewhere in this broad land of ours there actually was another tall, skinny twelve-year-old detective with a tree house office — but was it protected by a secret burglar alarm?

He was especially pleased with himself because he had been able to install the alarm while both Shirley and Thumbs were elsewhere. Thoughts of how he would surprise them with it tomorrow gave his melancholy face an almost merry expression as he grinned to himself. Roger's normal cast of countenance would not have been out of place in a funeral procession, but was no gauge of his true disposition. He happened to have eyebrows and eyes that slanted down at the corners, and a mouth that drooped at the corners as well, so that the average bloodhound looked cheerful by contrast. but this merely goes to show how appearances can be deceiving.

At the same time, the bloodhound look fitted him in one way. His old friend Sarge, the gardener out at Hessian Run Farm, called him the "boy bloodhound." Constable Mervin Stubbert, in a less friendly vein, called him "the nosiest kid in town," but then he was the village police officer, and was naturally resentful when Roger's amateur sleuthing outdid his own bumbling efforts. It was with good reason that the residents of East Widmarsh had given Roger the nickname of "Inspector." When anyone in the village had a mystery of any sort on his hands, Inspector

Tearle was quick to respond. Sometimes, much to Constable Stubbert's annoyance, Roger didn't even wait to be asked.

After a while his moonlit meditation was interrupted by the sound of his mother's voice coming up the stairs.

"Roger, is your light out?"

"Yes, Mom," he said virtuously.

"Are you in bed?"

He sighed. Mothers always ask one too many questions.

"No, Mom. I was just going."

"Well, get to bed, now. I want you to have some extra sleep. You've been staying up too late. Your sister's been asleep for an hour."

Shirley, that troublemaker. Sometimes it was a burden to have a twin sister. Even though they didn't look alike or act alike, their being exactly the same age made for this sort of difficulty.

"Okay, Mom. Good night."

Reaching under his desk, Roger closed a small electric switch, the kind called a knife switch. His burglar alarm was now on. He had already taken down the tree house ladder and put it in the garage for the night, so now his office was doubly protected. But if anyone did manage to climb up there, that someone would get quite a surprise. Let an intruder so much as set foot inside the tree house, and Roger would know it.

Closing his bedroom door, he reluctantly but duti-fully slipped into bed. He considered sleeping a waste of time, and often when a puzzling case was agitating his brain cells he had trouble dropping off. It was all very well for Shirley, all she ever thought about was eating. Unless she went to bed hungry, which was highly unlikely, she had nothing on her mind. Not so Inspector Tearle, however, when-ever something was afoot that demanded a solution.

At present, though, things were quiet in East Widmarsh. Nothing had happened since the old Fentriss house had burned down, and that had not re-mained a mystery for long. Soothed by thoughts of the added protection he had provided for his office, and smiling to himself as he imagined the fun he would have with Shirley and Thumbs in the morn-ing, Roger was soon snoozing peacefully.

CLANG-G-G-G!
Somewhere a bell was ringing! Roger came up from the black depths of a sound sleep like a swim-mer popping to the surface in a dark pond. His eyes flew open and he sat up, bewildered. Then his mind began to function. The burglar alarm! It had rung! Leaping out of bed, he grabbed a flashlight and rushed to the window. He sent a circle of light slid-ing across a shrouded window opening to the tarp that hung down over the doorway. It was fastened in place, undisturbed. Quickly Roger played the beam

over the lawn at the base of the tree. Nobody there. He snapped off the light and watched narrowly for any sign of movement in the yard. Nothing. The moon had long since gone down. It was pitch dark outside.

How could anyone climb up into the tree house without a ladder, and then, when the alarm bell went off, jump down and get away before Roger reached his window? All the doorway tarpaulin's ropes were still around their cleats. To get inside, an intruder would have had to unfasten at least the two bottom loops on each side. Anyone who jumped down when the alarm went off could hardly have turned around in midair and fastened the tarp behind him!

Roger glanced over his shoulder and listened, hoping that nobody else had been awakened. Shirley's room was across the hall at the back of the house, so that the tree house could be seen from her window too; but she was usually a sound sleeper. Their parents' room was at the other end of the hall. It was a lucky thing he had closed his door. Maybe the sound had not been quite loud enough, or lasted long enough, to awaken anyone else. He checked his bedside clock. Three o'clock! Who would be prowling around at three o'clock in the morning? He began to think that perhaps he had only dreamed the alarm had gone off. Still, he had to investigate.

Easing his door open, he crept silently down the stairs and made his way through the house to the back door. His flesh tingled as he peered out into the dark. Was anybody out there, somewhere in the shadows, or hiding behind the garage? Many a boy might have lost his nerve at this point, and turned back to wake up his father, but Inspector Tearle was made of sterner stuff. With him, fear was seldom a match for curiosity. After the briefest hesitation, and a slight gulp, he stole outside, gripping his long flashlight more like a war club than a torch. He did not snap it on. The heavy dew on the grass was icy on his bare feet, and the early morning chill made him shiver in his light pajamas. He walked to the foot of the big oak and stopped to look around, tingling again from the nape of his neck to the base of his spine. Stillness everywhere, and black night.

His eyes had adjusted to the darkness now. He could make out the blurred outlines of all the familiar objects in the back yard. The lawn chairs, the wrought-iron table, the birdbath. He stared up at the tree house. It was impossible for anyone to be inside now, and it seemed impossible that anyone could have *been* inside, but he had to check. Turning, he forced himself to walk back to the garage, where he kept his ladder. What if someone had slipped into the garage?

The overhead door was closed, but there was an ordinary door on the side. Opening it took the most nerve of all. Holding his flashlight at the ready, Roger turned the knob, pushed the door open, and snapped on the flash. He was ready to yell and run at the slightest provocation.

A sudden scurry inside all but scared that yell out of him. His flash caught a whisk of movement in a corner. Just in time he knew it was a field mouse. It took him a moment to get his breath back. He swept the beam this way and that, checking everything thoroughly. Nothing else stirred. He went in for the ladder. He had to turn off his light before he started outside, of course, and that was the worst moment of all, that moment of working the ladder around the car and out through the door in the suffocating black

stillness of the garage. After that, being outside was almost relaxing.

With exaggerated care he set the ladder into place against the tree house. Quickly climbing its eight rungs, he unhooked the rope loops from their cleats enough to work his head and flashlight inside the tree house. He snapped on the light, and his eyes went wide.

There on the floor, a couple of feet from the doorway, were a pair of footprints. Made by soles wet with dew, they stood out quite clearly. And just beyond them was a small pile of scraps of paper.

Footprints! It was impossible, yet there they were!

❧ 2

FOR A FEW SECONDS, Roger simply stared. Then he snapped off his flashlight and unfastened two more loops on the tarp. This done, he was able to slip inside.

CLANG-G-G-G!

Roger jumped like an angry cat. He all but leaped out of the tree house altogether, in his eagerness to stop that confounded clanging. He bounded back to doorway with such vigor that he lost his balance, swung around wildly in the folds of the doorway tarp as he hung onto a post, and stumbled down the ladder two steps before he could catch himself. The worst part of that was that he was off-center, and his pajama leg got caught over one of the sidepieces of the ladder.

13

Never had Inspector Tearle been more humiliated. To think he could forget about his own burglar alarm! The instant he stepped off the floor of the tree house, the alarm stopped, but the damage was done. Shirley's light had already gone on. He was still standing on the ladder, fighting his way out of the folds of the tarp, and trying to tug the torn leg of his pajamas loose, when a beam from his own window spotlighted him for all the world to see.

"Roger!" cried Shirley in girlish wonder. "What are you doing out there?"

He glared at her like some wild beast in a trap.

"Turn that flashlight off!" he ordered in a fury.

"Gee, you've torn your pajamas!" she commented, and Roger squeezed his eyes shut as he felt the last semblance of self-control slipping away from him. Sister murder! What prosecutor would dare call it anything but justifiable homicide, what judge fail to nod approval as Roger was carried out of the courtroom on the shoulders of a cheering jury?

"I know I've torn my pajamas! Now turn off that — Oh, boy!"

Roger sagged in limp defeat as the light in his room went on behind Shirley. Now here came their parents. It was fate. He was meant to drain the bitter cup to the last drop.

Clutching her robe about her, his mother stared out at him.

"Roger Tearle, what are you doing out there at this hour of the night?"

Pushing to the window between the ladies, his father took over.

"Roger, do you realize it's three o'clock in the morning?"

"Yes, Dad."

"Well, what was all that racket you were making?"

"My new burglar alarm."

"Your what?"

"I rigged a burglar alarm on the tree house."

"What?" cried Shirley. "When?"

"Listen, never mind all this now," interrupted Mr. Tearle, "just get down and come in here, before you wake up the whole neighborhood." A couple of lights had already gone on in windows across the street.

"I can't! I'm caught."

"Oh, for — Wait, I'll come out," snapped his father.

"No, never . . . mind." With a final desperate tug that involved another few inches of ripping, Roger got his pajama leg loose.

"Shirl, reach under my desk, you'll find a switch," he said in a glum voice. The whole surprise was shot now, anyway. "Open it."

"Why?"

"Oh, for Pete's sake, just do it! It controls my burglar alarm. I can't go inside my office till it's off."

"Roger, are you out of your mind?" asked his mother. "You come in the house this minute!"

"But, Mom, somebody was in my office! That's why the alarm went off. There's footprints, and I've got to measure them right away!"

"I found the switch," Shirley reported. "It's open."

"Good!" Roger darted inside. Yanking open the desk drawer, he seized a ruler and went madly to work measuring the footprints. Eight inches long, three and a half wide.

The ladder rattled, startling him so badly he dropped the ruler. A stern voice thundered up at him.

"Roger, did you hear your mother?"

"Yes, Dad, but — "

"Young man, if I have to come up there — Ow!"

Roger stuck his head out from under the tarp. His father seemed to be doing a one-legged dance on the lawn, also in his pajamas.

"What's the matter, Dad?"

"That cursed ladder of yours! It ran a splinter into my foot!"

"Gee, I'm sorry, Dad! Go on in, and I'll be right along as soon as I fasten the tarp and put the ladder away."

"If you're not in the house in one minute flat, you'll think you've got a burglar alarm in your britches!" threatened the injured man furiously as he limped away toward the house. Meanwhile Inspector Tearle was not letting this blessed reprieve go to waste. He had already turned back to work. Taking an envelope from his desk, he scooped the pile of paper scraps into it and stuffed the envelope into his pajama jacket pocket. Then he slipped outside, fastened the tarp, and dropped swiftly down the ladder.

"Must remember to sand these rungs tomorrow," he reminded himself, fingering them cautiously as he walked the ladder back to the garage on his shoulder. "They *are* getting a little splintery."

By the time he went inside, the family was assembled in the kitchen. His father was sitting in a captain's chair, gripping the arms like a man about to be tortured, while his mother held the damaged foot in her lap and prepared to take out the splinter with a needle. Shirley was watching avidly, and eating a few cookies to settle her nerves.

"Well! It's nice of you to drop by, Roger," said Mr. Tearle with heavy sarcasm, glaring at him. "Just what — Ow! Be careful!"

"Oh, you big baby, I *am* being careful," said Mrs. Tearle. "Hold still. It's almost out."

"Honest, Dad, it wasn't my fault," said Roger. "Somebody *was* in my office, and set off the alarm. It's fixed so that if anybody steps in, it goes off."

"Well, you must have rigged it wrong somehow.

Don't tell me someone was up there at three o'clock in the morning! Are you sure those footprints aren't some old ones of yours or Shirley's?"

"Those footprints were wet, Dad."

"Wet?"

"From the dew on the grass."

"Hmm. Well, still, it's mighty strange the fool thing went off the very first night you got it rigged up."

"Yes, it is strange," Inspector Tearle agreed thoughtfully.

"All I can say is — Ouch!"

"There we are. It's out." Mrs. Tearle held up the splinter on the end of her finger. Shirley inspected it with a critical eye.

"Why, gee, it's hardly anything," she scoffed, causing her father to transfer his glare to her for a change.

"For your information, it felt like a log!" he snapped, and swiveled his eyes around at each of them in turn. Then Mrs. Tearle giggled, and Shirley snorted behind her hand, and they all started laughing, and Mr. Tearle had to laugh at himself. He shook his head.

"The things you put me through, Roger! The things you put yourself through, for that matter," he added, surveying his son's ragged pajama leg. "You look like some castaway who's just crawled up on a desert island."

Next Mr. Tearle's tiny wound had to be dabbed with iodine, which he loudly assured them stung like blazes, and after that a strip of adhesive bandage was put on it, and then they all went back to bed. Roger was ordered to change his pajamas, which he did, pausing only to take the envelope out of his pajama jacket pocket and lay it on his work table. Soon the house was quiet again, and seventy-five per cent of its occupants were once more asleep. For the remaining twenty-five per cent, sleep was out of the question, of course. Every last brain cell at Inspector Tearle's command — and they were an awesome army — had been called out on emergency duty to consider the puzzle that had suddenly confronted him. An impossible trespass had been committed in his tree house office, and when apparent explanations proved to be impossible, then it was necessary to start searching for the unexpected possible.

Furthermore, there were those scraps of paper to investigate. He could hardly wait until he was sure everybody was asleep, so that he could get up, tiptoe over to his work table, turn on his lamp, and dump out the contents of the envelope.

The scraps were not hard to fit together. There were ink marks on some of them, and when he had put them together, the marks formed three words, printed in large size with a marking pen. Inspector

Tearle frowned angrily when he read their imperti-
nent challenge:

TRY, TRY
AGAIN

"Ha!" he muttered, as one or two things suddenly
fitted together in his teeming mind. He picked up a
ruler, found one of his sneakers under the bed, and
measured its length. Nine inches. An inch longer
than the footprints in the tree house. He walked to
the window and stood looking out into the darkness.
For some moments he stared across the dark fields and
woods behind the house, beyond which on a slight
rise stood Fieldcrest, the old Twyman place, recently
bought by a wealthy family named Milford.

There were two questions to be settled: how the
trick had been done, and who did it. Inspector Tearle
was not yet sure of the How, but he thought he knew
the Who.

❧ 3

"Look at those eyes!" said Mrs. Tearle when Roger came down to breakfast next morning. "I suppose you didn't sleep another wink all night."

"Sure, I did," he said. "I'm fine."

"You have shadows under your eyes," insisted his mother, and of course when you started with eyes as normally mournful-looking as Roger's and then put shadows under them as well, the result was enough to alarm any mother.

"Well, I feel fine, anyway."

His father appeared from the living room.

"I suppose you have the mystery all worked out," he said, giving his son a sharp look.

"I've got a few ideas," admitted Roger, "but I'll

have to do some checking first." His sad eyes twinkled as he watched his father across the room. "How's your foot, Dad? Gee, you hardly limp at all."

"Very funny," said Mr. Tearle, rapping Roger's head with a hard knuckle before he could duck out of the way. "My foot feels good enough to give you a kick in the pants, so watch out."

Shirley was already well into her second bowl of cereal, but she paused long enough to say, "I want to see how the burglar alarm works."

"You will, as soon as Thumbs gets here," said Roger. "At least I can still surprise *him* with it."

Thumbs was due in a few minutes, because every morning the three of them rode their bikes out to Hessian Run Farm to get the eggs they delivered all over the village. One of the many enterprises Roger had conceived in his diversified career was a deal with Mr. Chadburn to peddle the excess eggs produced on the farm. They had a daily egg route to take care of.

As soon as he had finished breakfast, Roger hurried out to put the tree house ladder in place and roll up all the tarps, assisted by Shirley.

"Now, come on, let's get upstairs before Thumbs shows up, and then you'll see something," he said, and they raced inside. When Thumbs appeared on his bike, they were standing at Roger's window.

"Hi, Thumbs. We'll be right down," called Roger.

"Listen, I left today's customer list on my desk. Climb up and get it, will you?"

"Sure." Thumbs parked his bike against the tree and started up the ladder. His foot slipped on the third rung and he barked his shin on it, but then that was Thumbs all over. His awkwardness had won him his nickname, which was short for All Thumbs. He was so used to bumps and bruises that he seldom let them slow him down any. He gave his shin a quick rub and continued on up the ladder, and stepped into the tree house.

CLANG-G-G-G!

He whirled around wildly.

"Hey! What's that?"

"Shut it off, Shirl," ordered Roger, and Shirley pulled the switch open. The clanging stopped. "That's our new burglar alarm."

"What? A burglar alarm? Great! How's it work?"

"Now let me climb up there," said Shirley, and went outside. After Thumbs had climbed down and she had climbed up and set the alarm going again, Roger turned it off and joined them to explain. First he pointed to the telephone wire that ran from the tree house over to his window and down the side of the house to the kitchen.

"If you'll take a good look, you can see there's another wire wrapped around the telephone wire now."

"It runs out from Roger's window and down the

24

side of the tree house and underneath," said Shirley, who had already had it pointed out to her.

"Now climb up the ladder and look underneath and you'll see where it goes," said Roger.

There was only a few inches' clearance between the bottom of the tree house and the big limb that was its main support. One strand of the new wire ran to a copper stud fastened to the underside of the floor. The other ran to a second copper stud fastened onto a strip of spring steel nailed to the tree. The two studs were almost touching.

"You see?" said Roger. "The instant anybody steps on the floor, his weight bends it enough to make them touch. You two stand on the ladder and watch the studs when I step inside."

The demonstration was convincing.

"They touch, all right," said Thumbs. "The spring even bends down a little."

"Well, that's how it works," said Roger, "but wait till you hear what happened last night."

Shirley's pony tail pranced around gleefully as she threw her head back to laugh.

"You should have seen Roger hanging out here with his pajamas all torn!" she said. "Let *me* tell it, Roger!"

"Now, wait a minute —"

"Well, I *saw* it all. You only *did* it."

Between them, with considerable bickering and

many interruptions, the story finally got told. When Thumbs had heard it all, he shook his head in amazement.

"It's impossible," he said. "It couldn't have happened."

Inspector Tearle nodded.

"That's right. It couldn't have happened the way it *seemed* to happen. So when you're up against the impossible, what do you do? You look for the possible. Now, anybody who put any weight on these floorboards would have set off my alarm. But nobody could have been in here and got away before I saw him, once the alarm went off. That's an impossibility. Now, what's a possibility?"

Shirley's face brightened. There were certain programs on television that she never missed. She volunteered her version of a possibility.

"A creature from outer space who's weightless!"

Roger and Thumbs exchanged a long, male stare that commented eloquently on the female mind.

"I was standing at my window, and I didn't see a single spaceship," said Roger with what was intended to be a crushing tone. As usual, it failed to crush Shirley. She looked down her nose at both of them.

"You can laugh, but you'll be laughing on the other side of your stupid faces one of these days," she declared passionately. "Just because our dopey Air Force says every Unidentified Flying Object is marsh gas or something silly doesn't prove — "

"Shirley, do you mind?" snarled Inspector Tearle, who was in no mood to hear about little green men from other planets. "If you'll just shut up, I think I can prove this was a *local* job."

Brother and sister glared at each other for a moment. Then Shirley shrugged.

"Oh, all right. Go ahead. But what burns me up is the way you act as if it couldn't possibly be — "

"*Quiet!*" shouted Inspector Tearle. "The creature that did this job wasn't weightless, and if you'll give me a chance I'll explain how those footprints got here."

Rising from the only chair — the others were sitting on the floor — he started down the ladder. At eye level with the floor he stopped to add a comment.

"Remember, the grass was wet with dew," he said, and then dropped on down the ladder. He walked to an outside water faucet, turned it on, pulled off his sneakers, and held their soles under the water. He returned with the sneakers, stood on the ladder, and reached into the tree house with a sneaker in each hand. He gently touched them to the floor and took them away again.

"There's your footprints."

The others stared at him.

"Of course, it was easy to reach in and dump the scraps of paper on the floor," he added. "Whoever it was only had to unfasten the bottom loops on the

27

tarp to do all that. Then after he had fastened everything again, he came down and set off the alarm."

"Set it off? How?"

"Well, he could have done it in a number of ways.
But first I'll tell you *who* I think did it."

Inspector Tearle had his audience in the hollow of
his hand now. They stared at him breathlessly.

"Who?"

Still standing on the ladder, he pointed a dramatic
forefinger sideways in the direction of Fieldcrest.

"The Firebug!"

🌸 4

IF INSPECTOR TEARLE had been onstage, he could not have created a more dramatic impression.

"Hazy Milford?"

"That little creep?" snorted Thumbs.

"Hays Milford," nodded Roger, giving him his true name. Because of his strange ways, the nickname had been almost inevitable.

"What makes you think it was him?" asked Shirley.

"Well, first of all, everyone knows he likes to prowl around at night any time he can. He's been seen out at all hours."

"He's a night crawler," said Thumbs.

"And he's tricky. He likes to play tricks."

"Like burning down houses," said Thumbs. It

29

was Hazy Milford and a couple of no-good older boys he had been spending his time with who had been seen in the abandoned house, the old Fentriss place, the night it burned down. Mr. Milford paid the property owner a lot of money, and the charges against Hazy were dropped, but everybody knew he had set the old house on fire, and nobody at school had much to do with him.

Roger continued to build his case.

"Next, he came by yesterday on his bike while I was working on the alarm. I didn't give him any encouragement, but he stopped and watched me for a while."

"Did he ask you what you were doing?"

"Yes. I just said I was fixing something, and after that I ignored him, and finally he went away. But he must have figured out for himself what I was doing."

"Okay, it sounds like he could be the one, all right — but how did he do it? How did he climb up here without a ladder, and get away afterward?"

"And how did he set off the alarm?" added Shirley.

"One thing at a time. Thumbs, remember those physical fitness tests they put us through at school in the spring?"

"Do I? They had my tongue hanging out."

"Remember how we all had to climb a rope hand-over-hand? And remember who was especially good at it?"

"Sure I do! That little monkey Hazy! But why shouldn't he be, he practices all the time in his own yard — Hey!" Thumbs got the idea. "You mean, that's how he did it! He threw a rope over a limb and climbed up here that way!"

"What did he tie it to?" asked Shirley.

"He probably took one end all the way around the trunk. Then he climbed the rope, put the scraps of paper inside, and marked the floor with his sneaker soles, while he was hanging on the rope."

From a pocket in his shorts Roger took a piece of cardboard on which he had pasted the scraps of paper.

"When I put these together, here's what I got."

The others examined the card eagerly.

"Try, try again!"

"He's a little smart aleck," said Roger. "Oh, and that's another point, too, the fact that he's little. I measured those footprints. They're an inch shorter than mine, and my feet aren't particularly big."

"What about the alarm, though?" said Shirley. "How did he set it off?"

But Inspector Tearle was not one to let all his deductions out of the bag at once.

"Well, I have a theory about that, but I want to spring it on Hazy first when we get there this morning with the eggs." Fieldcrest was on their route. Roger glanced at his electric wristwatch. "Come on, let's get going out to the farm."

Being used to their leader's methods, his assistants did not waste time trying to worm anything more out of him. They were shortly pedaling their bikes along the village streets and across the back fields of Hessian Run Farm. As usual, Roger led the way, because as usual he was the most desperately eager to get to the next place he was going.

The owner of the farm, Mr. Chadburn, was a millionaire financier and chicken fancier who raised prize fowls as a hobby, but had a tenant farmer named Zoltan to do the work. That morning Zoltan had the cartons of eggs all ready for them when they arrived. They strapped cartons into wire baskets fore and aft on their bikes and took off on their route. Half an hour later, after five or six stops, they reached Fieldcrest.

When it came to their scale of living, the Milfords even outdid Mr. Chadburn. They not only had a cook and a gardener, but a married couple who worked as their chauffeur and maid. Besides the house, which was a rambling Victorian mansion with at least twenty-five rooms, there was a gardener's cottage and a long, low stable that had been converted into a garage. The garage had room for four cars, with a special stall partitioned off from the rest in which Mr. Milford's magnificent antique automobile was kept. Next to the special stall was a storeroom that was used by Fidel the gardener.

As it turned out, Roger and his assistants picked

an interesting moment to arrive. They were just in time to watch the antique car, a Stutz Bearcat, being loaded into a van. Gleaming with canary yellow paint, it was perfect in every detail, from its two tan-colored bucket seats to its wooden-spoked wheels. Being an open roadster built along the general lines of a racer, it had no top. In the driver's seat sat its proud owner himself, with the motor running, while Martin the chauffeur and another man adjusted two steel tracks in front of the wheels. The tracks ran from the ground up to the back end of the truck. A small, sharp-faced boy was standing near the car — too near, it seemed, to suit his father.

"Get out of the way, Hays," snapped Mr. Milford. "Stand back!"

"There he is," muttered Thumbs as they stopped their bikes near the kitchen door of the house.

"Remember, now, one of us has got to stay close to the bikes at all times," Roger reminded them. With Hazy around, this was standard procedure. They figured he might decide it would be a funny joke to "accidentally" dump over a bike loaded with fresh eggs.

"All right, that looks good. Here we go!" said Mr. Milford confidently, and as they watched he slowly and masterfully drove the old car up the tracks and into the truck. It was something not everybody would have wanted to try, but Mr. Milford was said to think he was good at everything, and to be right most of the time. Among other things, he held several records as a hunter and a fisherman.

Of course, being the inquisitive sort of person he was, Roger already knew where the car was going. It was being taken to a shop that specialized in antique car repairs, to have some work done on its front axle. He had gotten that information from Martin a couple of days ago.

"Nice work, sir," said Martin, as Mr. Milford appeared at the back end of the enclosed van.

"Nothing to it," said the big, athletic man, jumping down to the ground and dusting his hands. "Be sure you brace those wheels solidly, and pad her up good, and then get rolling."

"Hey, Dad, why can't I go with them?" asked Hazy, and his father turned on him impatiently.

"Hays, I told you, I don't want you anywhere near this car ever again, and I meant it."

"Aw, that firecracker was only a joke. It didn't hurt anything."

"Well, your jokes are going to hurt *you* until you learn better. You wait till you get to military school this fall, my boy, and you'll find out where jokes can get you," said Mr. Milford, and strode away toward the house. The way Hazy looked as he watched his father go gave Roger a cold feeling all the way to his bones.

He took three cartons of eggs inside to the cook, and she said, "We won't be needing so many eggs for a while, Inspector. The Milfords are flying to Europe for three weeks day after tomorrow, and I'll be on vacation myself while they're gone."

"That so? Is Hazy going with them?"

"Oh, no." The cook glanced across the kitchen at Lucy the maid and chuckled. "Lucy and Martin will be taking care of Master Hays," she said, while Lucy sighed and rolled up her eyes. Roger was not surprised to hear that Hazy was being left home. For one thing, Mrs. Milford was not his mother. She was Mr. Milford's second wife, and it was well known that she and Hazy did not get along at all.

When Roger went outside again, Hazy was still hanging around the van, watching the men work. His sharp face seemed to grow sharper and foxier, and his eyes were shifty but amused, as Roger walked over to him. Thumbs and Shirley wheeled their bikes closer to listen.

"Hi, Hazy," said Roger. "Been doing any climbing and fishing lately?"

Hazy put his head on one side and laughed in a creepy way he had. He looked as if it hurt him, and his laughter didn't make any sound. Between the way he laughed and his squeaky, scratchy voice, he was a real weird one.

"Climbing and fishing?" he said. "No, why?"

"Well, somebody climbed a rope up to our tree house last night about three o'clock. Then after he'd put some fake footprints inside — small ones — " Roger added pointedly, glancing down at Hazy's feet, "and after he'd dumped some scraps of paper on the floor, he stood under the tree with something long, like one of his father's casting rods, something with a metal tip, and he touched two copper points with it, and that made my new burglar alarm go off."

Hazy's small, close-set eyes stared up at Roger unblinkingly.

"He did? Say, you're pretty smart to figure all that out. Did you catch him?"

"No. But he'd better stay away from now on, or he'll wish he had."

"He sure will," growled Thumbs, and glowered down at Hazy so threateningly that the smaller boy's cocky expression began to wilt around the edges.

"Okay, we can't waste any more time here," said Roger. "Let's get going."

They swung onto their bikes and rode away down the drive. They had nearly reached the gate before Hazy finally said anything.

"How's your pajamas?" he shouted, and ran laughing toward the house.

"Why, that little crumb!" said Roger, jamming to a stop and then, when he had a foot braced against the ground, twisting around to look back. As he did, he noticed Fidel the gardener coming out of the storeroom. Fidel was a squat dark man. Not even Roger had been able to make friends with him. He kept to himself. He stood watching Hazy for a moment, and his eyes narrowed under his heavy black eyebrows. Then he turned and carefully locked the storeroom door behind him.

"I don't think Fidel likes Hazy any better than the rest of us do," remarked Roger. "Still, I've got to be fair — I haven't noticed Fidel liking *anybody*."

All in all, Fieldcrest was not Roger's idea of a pleasant place, for all its luxury.

❧ 5

FOR A WEEK, life had been quiet again. The only case
that had come Inspector Tearle's way was a case of
indigestion. He had gotten some kind of bug, and it
had laid him low for a day. Worse yet, it had picked
the very day when a carnival showed up over at
Burgessville, the largest town near East Widmarsh.
Their parents had planned to take him and Shirley
over, and Thumbs was going too. Now he was forced
to stay home in bed while the others went without
him. He was feeling better, but his mother refused
to let him get up and go to a carnival after being sick
in bed all day.

Setting aside the piece of dry toast he had been
nibbling, Roger indulged in a great groan of self-
pity. Then anger took over. He was almost tempted

to change his plans for the future. Instead of a scientist, he would become a doctor and wipe out disease! He'd show those bugs! But then, after a moment, he sighed, and shook his head, and gave up a medical career. It wasn't really what he wanted, bugs or no bugs.

He picked up a book and tried to read, but his active imagination would not let him. It kept tormenting him with bright pictures of all the fun Shirley and Thumbs were having on the Ferris wheel and the roller coaster and in the fun house. That Shirley! She ate three times what he did, yet no bug every successfully attacked *her* digestion.

A gentle breeze stirred the curtains of his open window, wafting in the pleasant scents of a perfect summer evening from the darkness outside. It *would* have to be a perfect night. Might at least have rained!

He glanced at the mail on his work table. Roger got most of the mail in the Tearle household, since he was constantly sending off for things, or writing hither and yon for information, or getting involved in such matters as postal chess tournaments. Two or three postal chess cards were waiting for his attention right now, and a lawyer in Madison, Wisconsin, was in for a nasty surprise when he received Roger's reply to his latest move.

A box from a firm that dealt in magicians' equipment was the largest item in that day's mailbag. No doubt it contained an object known as the Swami's Card Box which he had sent for some time ago. When Shirley had brought it up earlier in the day, he had been too miserable to take any interest in it. Now, however, he decided he might feel equal to opening it.

Swinging his long skinny legs over the side of his sickbed, Roger crossed the room to his table, but he never touched the box. As he came near the window, a reddish glow in the distance drew him to it with a rush. He gripped the windowsill and stared.

Fire!

Even as he watched, flames leaped higher on the rise above the fields and woods behind the house. The fire was over at Fieldcrest!

To watch Roger leap into his shorts and T shirt, nobody would have thought he was an invalid. Ordinarily he would not have wasted time with anything further, but now, thinking ahead, as usual, he stopped to yank on his sneakers, reminding himself that a fire was nothing to be around barefooted.

"What has that little creep done now, set fire to his own house?" he wondered as he hurried outside. In the distance, as he sprinted across the dark fields, fire truck sirens began to wail. Ahead of him the flames were a ruddy glare in the sky, and he could hear their roar and crackle. When he reached the woods at the foot of the hill, following a path he knew well, something rustled in the bushes, startling

him, but outside of shying to one side for a stride or two he didn't let it stop him. Soon he reached the stone wall that marked the boundary of the Fieldcrest property. Everything around him stood out plain as day now because of the angry glow overhead. Scrambling over the low wall, he hurried on up the path, panting now from the exertion, and burst into the open on the broad side lawn.

Coming into the open was like stepping into a blast furnace. It was the garage that was burning. A fire truck and two cars were just arriving. A dozen men were shouting at once as they scurried around the edges of the fire. Their figures made black silhouettes against the flames.

Roger's quick glance took in a dozen things at once. The house, which was a good hundred yards from the garage, seemed to be out of danger, and the gardener's cottage, equally far away in his direction, was safe if no embers fell on it. Roger was just in time to see Fidel slip inside the door of his cottage. Why was he going in, when he should have been coming out, if anything? Roger's first impulse was to draw back into the woods for fear Fidel would notice him, but then he changed his mind. Why shouldn't Fidel see him, so long as Roger didn't act as if he were spying on him? He ran forward across the lawn, careful not to glance in the direction of the cottage as he passed it.

There was a crash, and a burst of sparks sprayed up into the sky like fireworks as a section of the garage roof fell in. Firemen were frantically paying out fire hose now, running it back to a hydrant alongside the driveway. More sirens wailed nearer and nearer, bigger and better fire trucks arrived. Constable Mervin Stubbert swerved up the driveway in the village's lone police car, not more than a minute ahead of a State Police car. The village constable began to bustle around, getting in the way of various firemen and otherwise asserting his authority. Presently he noticed Roger.

"What are you doing here? Someone down to the post office said you were sick in bed," he declared, disappointed. "Now, you stay out of the way and keep behind the police lines, do you hear?" he ordered importantly, and hurried off to trip over a fire hose.

Fidel had reappeared over at his cottage, and was throwing a bucket of water up on his roof. Certainly that made good sense, because the breeze had freshened and was carrying embers in that direction. Here was a chance to check up on the gardener. Roger ran over to the cottage.

"Hi, Fidel. Want some help?"

The squat man's beady eyes flickered at him. But then he nodded.

"Okay. Fill buckets," he said, and led the way

inside. The cottage was none too neatly kept, and had an earthy smell about it, but nothing of special interest caught Inspector Tearle's busy eyes.

The next few minutes were such strenuous ones, especially for a boy who had just left his sickbed, that Roger wished he had stayed away from Fidel. Now he had trapped himself with him, and nothing he observed concerning the cottage or the way Fidel acted seemed significant. Yet he couldn't leave, because embers kept falling on the roof, and Fidel needed his help. Roger carried out his share of the buckets, and Fidel threw their contents on the roof with a powerful twist of his broad shoulders.

Meanwhile the hoses and some chemical equipment began to bring the fire under control. For that matter, the garage had nearly burned to the ground, so that after a while there was not much left to burn. Finally Fidel stopped for a look.

"Okay," he said, putting down an empty bucket, and with that he walked away toward the fire. Not a glance back at Roger, not a word of thanks. For a moment Roger stared after him, outraged. Then he had to chuckle.

"Well, you're welcome, señor!" he muttered, and hurried back to the fire himself. Now he could pick out Martin the chauffeur standing in the middle of a circle of men, watching the flames gradually die down as streams of water hissed over them.

"If you ask me, Martin did a great job of saving

two cars from a fire like that!" Constable Stubbert was saying. Roger had already noticed that the Milford's Bentley and Jaguar were on the lawn beside the drive.

"I wish I could have saved the station wagon, too," said Martin, "but by that time it was getting a little too hot in there. Worst of all, I never had a chance at the Stutz, because that's where the fire was the worst."

Roger was appalled by this last comment. He had just been thinking how lucky it was that the Stutz was away being worked on. Undaunted by his elders, Roger stepped forward to put in his two cents' worth.

"Gee, Martin, was the Stutz in there?"

The chauffeur glanced down at him with eyes that were bloodshot under singed eyebrows, and nodded grimly.

"We brought it back yesterday!" he said. "Of all the rotten luck!"

Roger turned to peer at the flickering ruins of the garage. It was hard to make out details in the fiery mess that was left, but now that he looked he could see two car radiators under a tangle of blackened timbers. The broad hood of the station wagon and the old-fashioned squared-off fenders of the Stutz Bearcat were unmistakable. And it was the loss of the fine old antique car that made the fire a terrible thing.

"Hey, you! Beat it!" Constable Stubbert had noticed the presence of his local competition. "I thought I told you to stay behind the fire lines!"

"Oh, leave the Inspector alone, Merv," said one of the other men. They all knew Roger, in fact several of them were customers on his egg route. "Maybe he can put his nose to the ground and find that Milford kid."

"Hazy?" said Roger. "Where is he?"

"That's what everybody would like to know. He was out here when the fire started — Martin's wife saw him — but he ran away and disappeared."

"You'd better start looking for him, Merv," said Martin.

"Sooner that boy's locked up for good, the better, if you ask me," said another man in a hard voice.

"Now, wait a minute," said Martin. "We don't know for sure that he started this fire — "

"Ha! We know he's a firebug, and that's good enough for me!"

"I'll get the state boys to help," said Constable Stubbert, suddenly mindful of his duties. "We'll find him! He can't have gone far."

Roger stared at the fire with blank eyes, seeing something else. He was remembering the way Hazy had looked, watching his father walk away, that day the Stutz was being loaded into the van. Had he set the fire to spite his father? Anyone who would do a thing like that really ought to be locked up. He was sick in the head.

As he watched and listened, however, Roger began to have problems with his own head. It was swimming. He realized he had better go somewhere and sit down for a minute. All this activity and exertion after being sick in bed had caught up with him. He tottered away and collapsed in the grass, unnoticed by the others. He had to rest for quite a while before he felt like getting up and making his way home at a much slower pace than the dead run he had used in coming to the fire. He actually staggered a few times on his way home. He was very glad to see his own back yard again.

As he was crossing it, a car came down the side street and stopped, and he found himself blinking in the sudden, startling blaze of a searchlight.

"You again!" said an annoyed voice.

"Hi, Constable."

"Roger, you look puny. Get to bed!"

The car jerked away down the street, leaving him in darkness. With a feeling that he wasn't making it a minute too soon, he walked in the back door, flipped on the lights, and sagged into a kitchen chair.

"Whew!" said Inspector Tearle. He consulted his stomach, and found it to be in reasonably good order. "Maybe what I need is a glass of milk."

Ordinarily he had no high regard for this beverage, but there were times when it could be a restorative. After a moment's rest, he tottered to the refrigerator and poured himself a glass.

He was sitting down again, drinking his milk, when an incredible thing happened.

A buzzer sounded on the other side of the room.

It was the buzzer connected to a special telephone he had installed for his mother's convenience.

The other end of the telephone line was connected to a receiver in the tree house.

For a few seconds Inspector Tearle stared across the kitchen at the buzzer, as though daring it to repeat its summons.

It did.

Staggering to his feet, he crossed the kitchen and lifted the receiver.

"Hello?"

"Come out here," whispered a scratchy voice.

There was no mistaking it. It was the voice of Hazy Milford.

❧ 6

INSPECTOR TEARLE'S CAREER had been studded with astonishing moments, but nothing surpassed this one. At first he clutched his forehead and wondered if the evening had been too much for him. Was he delirious? Was he hearing things?

"Hazy?"

"Yes."

"What are you doing in my tree house? How did you get there? What — "

He paused and pulled himself together. It was no time to babble. He had a firebug on his hands, and the sooner he got rid of him, the better. Clear thinking and fast action, that was the ticket.

"Now, listen, Hazy. Stay right there. I'll be out in just a minute."

But Hazy read his mind. The squeaky voice was low and urgent.

"Don't call the police," he said. "I didn't do it."

"You what?"

"I don't know who started that fire, but I didn't. Whoever did knew everybody would think it was me, but I didn't do it."

Roger frowned. The little creep was lying, of course. Anybody sick enough to start a fire like that would be able to lie like a streak.

"Come out here and I'll tell you what happened," Hazy urged him.

The only sensible thing to do was to call the police, rather than get involved with Hazy Milford in any way. But now Roger's curiosity, always easily aroused, was rampant. The chance to be the first to talk to Hazy, before the police got hold of him, was tempting. Too tempting.

"Okay, I'm coming out," he said, and hung up.

A minute earlier he had been wondering if he had strength enough left to crawl upstairs to bed, but now he sprang into action again. He hurried outside to the foot of the big oak and stared up at the tree house. Even then he reminded himself to be on guard. The important thing was not to be taken in by Hazy's story, no matter how convincing he made it sound.

A hand appeared from inside, groped for the bottom loops on the doorway tarp, and unfastened them on each side. A rope end dropped down to him.

"Quick, climb up!" whispered Hazy. "I've got it tied around a post."

"Are you kidding? I'll get the ladder," said Roger, and stalked off toward the garage. In his condition, he was not about to take any physical fitness tests. He hadn't been too hot a rope climber, even when he was well.

The overhead door was open. He brought out the ladder and set it in place. Even that much effort made him feel weak in the knees again. He climbed up, hooked the bottom of the tarp up out of the way, and stared at the white face that seemed to be float-

ing dimly in the darkness of the interior, where Hazy crouched in a corner. Still standing on the ladder, looking in, Roger asked,

"Where did you get the rope?"

"I found it in your garage."

"Boy! You make yourself at home, don't you? What happened to my burglar alarm?"

"I pulled one of the wires loose before I climbed in."

Outrage upon outrage! It was enough to make a fellow jump down and go call the police at once!

"I had to," added Hazy.

"Well, you've got some nerve! Why did you come here, anyway?"

"I got the idea when you ran past me in the woods."

Roger remembered the sudden rustle that had startled him.

"Was that you I heard?"

"Yes. I decided to hide here, because nobody would think of looking for me here, and because I couldn't think of anybody else who would help me."

"What do you mean, help you?" Roger climbed inside and crouched down opposite the strange boy. "What made you think I'd help you?"

"Well, you're the hotshot detective around here," said Hazy in a mocking voice, and yet with overtones of respect. "Everybody calls you Inspector. You're always finding out things for people. You're pretty good too. Look at the way you figured out my trick with the fishing rod."

Such flattery was heady stuff, and like all outstanding detectives Inspector Tearle had his share of vanity.

"Child's play," he snapped, doing his best to fight off a severe attack of self-admiration, with all its softening effects.

"Well, anyway, so now you've got to help me, and find out who started the fire," declared Hazy.

He paused, and his tone of voice lost all of its smart aleck quality. It became the voice of a boy who was scared and lonely.

"I've got to have *somebody* on my side before they grab me."

There was a genuine ring to this simple statement that took Roger by surprise. Was it possible? . . .

"But why should anybody else want to burn down your garage?"

"Don't ask me."

"Naturally, everybody's going to think you did it because you were mad at your father," said Roger, to see what reaction he would get.

Once again, what he got had a genuine ring to it that shook him up.

"I hate my father," Hazy said flatly, "but if I wanted to get back at him I wouldn't do it that way.

I wouldn't burn down a garage with a Stutz Bear-cat in it. You can bet he won't feel any worse about that than I do."

The way his voice trembled made one thing suddenly plain: no matter how he might feel about other people, Hazy had loved that antique car. Roger listened to him with a growing sense of alarm. He was beginning to believe the little monster, and that could be dangerous.

He cleared his throat.

"Okay, let's say you didn't do it. Then who did, and why?"

"I told you, I don't know."

"I'm not asking you, I'm asking myself."

Now the analytical mind of Inspector Tearle swung into high gear.

"Let's think about the possibilities. Does anybody hate you enough to do it just to get you in trouble?"

In the darkness Hazy seemed to be laughing his painful, soundless laugh.

"Well, I'm not everybody's favorite, but I can't think of anybody who'd go that far."

"Fidel? Have you ever done him a real dirty trick?"

"Hmm," said Hazy, and Roger understood at once that Fidel had not been spared. "Well, not too bad. Still, with Fidel you never know."

"Where did he come from?"

"My father picked him up on one of his hunting trips, down in South America somewhere."

"What did he keep in that storeroom in the garage?"

"Who knows? Gardening stuff, of course, but . . . He never let anybody in there, but nobody. Not even Martin."

"What I'm getting at is, somebody could have burned down the garage to destroy something that was in it."

"Say! Now you're talking," said Hazy eagerly. "Why, he could have had anything in there. A dead body, or . . ."

Hazy stopped, excited.

"Wow!" he murmured.

"Now, not so fast," said Inspector Tearle sternly. "We'll know tomorrow if there are any dead bodies in the wreckage — "

"Charred beyond recognition," said Hazy, rolling the stock phrase around on his tongue.

"You've been reading too many mystery stories."

"Well, all the same, I saw a funny thing just the other night. I saw two men come to Fidel's cottage, and later I saw them all go in the storeroom together."

Inspector Tearle's scoffing air faltered. He stared at the small dim face in the darkness.

"I suppose now you're going to tell me only two men came back out."

"No, they all came out again a few minutes later. But then the two men sort of sneaked away, and they were both carrying something. Some kind of packages. It was — well, there was funny business going on, all right."

Roger's mind was in a whirl. He no longer knew what to think. For all he knew, Hazy might be making up all this stuff about Fidel. And yet, what good would that do him? And if he wasn't making it up, then it ought to be looked into.

"Listen, let me tell you what happened, from the beginning," said Hazy.

Roger glanced outside uneasily.

"Okay, but make it fast. My family went over to the carnival in Burgessville, and they might come home any time now. And besides that, I wouldn't want another police car to come by and see the ladder up. They're out looking for you."

"I know. I heard Stubbert stop. I almost called to you when you were down in the yard, coming home. I clammed up just in time when old Merv put the light on you."

The picture forced a snicker out of Roger.

"That's great! There was old Merv sliding around, and here you were all the time."

"He'd flip if he knew," agreed Hazy. "But why didn't you go to the carnival?"

"I was sick in bed all day, so I had to stay home."

"Oh. Well, the carnival was why I was waiting

around out by the garage in the first place. When the fire started, I mean. Martin was going to come out at nine o'clock and take me over there. That was my bribe for being good and not making any trouble," he said, and Roger could sense more than see the jeering grin that went with the explanation. "I went out a little ahead of time and hung around near the station wagon, waiting."

Already, as he listened, Inspector Tearle was putting himself in Hazy's shoes. He knew just how he must have felt. Hazy couldn't wait to get going. He went out and hung around the garage, so that when Martin came out they wouldn't have to waste a minute.

"Pretty soon I noticed some smoke coming out from under the door where the Stutz is kept. I'd hardly seen it before there was a sort of explosion inside, and the door nearly blew off in my face. Then everything was on fire. I started to turn and run toward the house, but then I panicked. All I could think of was that nobody would believe I hadn't started the fire. I don't even remember how I got there, but the next thing I knew I was hiding in the woods."

Inspector Tearle was still in Hazy's shoes, more firmly than ever. They might be sneakers a size or so smaller than his own, but he managed the trick. Now he was a small, strange, unpopular boy who was known as a firebug, a boy whose father was three thousand miles away and wouldn't have trusted him anyway, a boy left in the care of servants and without a friend in the world. What was left for him but to run away and hide in the woods?

Roger's head was swimming again. He shook it hard, and came back to the present, back to the dark tree house, with a creepy boy he didn't even like crouched in one corner, telling him a story it was hard to believe, the wildest story he'd ever heard. He felt so weak that cold sweat was standing out on his forehead. He knew enough about law to know that he could end up in Juvenile Court over at the county seat as an accessory after the fact, and be in big trouble, if he got mixed up with a firebug. But he also knew that if he didn't help Hazy Milford, nobody else would.

Here was a case that went far beyond anything he had ever experienced. This was no Grimshaw Campstool Case, or Chilton Watch Case. It even made the dark doings out at Hessian Run Farm, a case forever sealed in his secret files, seem minor. So what could he do? Was he a detective, or wasn't he? Was he going to be Roger the Chickenhearted and play it safe, or was he going to be Inspector Tearle and take a chance?

"Okay, Hazy," said Inspector Tearle, "I'm going to get you a sleeping bag. You'll need it out here before morning."

🪷 7

Hurrying as fast as he could, Roger fetched a sleeping bag from his closet and took it out to Hazy. Every second he was afraid he would see the headlights of the family car turn into the drive just in time to catch him in the act. In spite of how feeble he was feeling by then, he carried the ladder to the garage at a trot, and sprinted from there to the house.

By that time he was so shaky that his teeth chattered as he all but crawled up the stairs to his room. He would have given anything simply to fall into bed as he was, but he forced himself to get back into his pajamas. And for once, despite the engrossing challenge facing him, body overcame mind. He was sleeping the sleep of exhaustion before his head touched the pillow.

The next time he opened his eyes, bright strips of sunlight showed around the edges of the window shade his mother had pulled down. He knew at once he had slept long past his usual early hour for rising. Even now, he might have stayed asleep, but something had startled him awake. Before he had time to do more than wonder what it was, he heard it again.

It was the rattle of the tree house ladder being set into place!

Roger reached the window in one convulsive leap and ran up the window shade so abruptly that it whirled at the top with the rat-tat-tat of a machine gun. Halfway up the ladder, Shirley was so startled she nearly sprang into space.

"Shirley!" hissed Roger. "What are you doing?"

"Why, I'm going to get today's egg list."

"Wait a minute! Stay out of there! I — I've got a surprise, and you'll spoil it. Come down! I'll be right there!"

Downstairs raced Roger, praying that his mother would not be in the kitchen to stop him from going outside. The kitchen was empty. He hurried out, and ran into sisterly disapproval.

"What are you doing out here in your pajamas? Besides, Mom said you're to stay in bed — "

"Where is she?"

"She's driving Daddy to work, and when she gets home she's going to drive us around with the eggs,

because Thumbs and I couldn't carry them all on our bikes."

"Good. I'll get the list."

Roger hurried up the ladder, undid the bottom loops of the tarp, and climbed inside. With his finger to his lips, he frowned a warning at Hazy, who was sitting up in his sleeping bag. Hazy nodded silently. Roger took the day's egg route list from the files and climbed down the ladder.

"What's your big secret?" Shirley asked suspiciously.

"I'll tell you later. Hurry, let's get inside before Mom comes back."

Once he had reached the safety of the kitchen, Roger sank into a chair and relaxed.

"Whew!" He took stock of himself. "Well! I feel pretty good," he discovered, "and I'm hungry!"

He fixed himself some breakfast, and Shirley had some more with him.

"How was the carnival, Shirl?"

"Great!" She told him about all the things they had seen, what rides they had taken, what they had bought to eat, and so on. Then her eyes lighted up with important news. "But guess what else happened last night while you were asleep! The Milfords' garage burned down over at Fieldcrest!"

Having had to hear about all he had missed at the carnival, Roger took a certain pleasure now in replying, "I know. I was there."

Shirley's reaction was satisfactorily envious.

"What? You were there?"

"Yes. I went over and watched it."

"Oh, you always have all the luck! It must have been the best fire we've ever had! I suppose you also know that Hazy Milford started it and ran away, and is still missing?"

"Yes, I know that too," said Roger in as infuriatingly pompous a tone as possible. Shirley fumed.

"Oh, if you weren't sick I'd belt you one! How did you know that?"

"I heard about it when I was over watching the fire."

"You were supposed to stay in bed!"

"Oh, sure. Would you have?"

"Well . . . no, but . . . Oh, here comes Mom!" The car stopped in the driveway. Mrs. Tearle came in.

"Well, good morning, dear! You must be feeling better," she said, kissing Roger and checking his forehead with her hand. "But I want you to get back in bed as soon as you've finished your breakfast."

Roger grinned up at her sheepishly.

"Shirley's mad because I saw the fire last night and she missed it."

"Roger! Do you mean you went over there?"

"Well, gee, Mom, it looked like the whole place was burning up, so I had to walk over and see."

"Ha! The day you walk anywhere, I want a box seat to watch! I suppose you went tearing over like a madman," she said worriedly, feeling his forehead again. "I suppose I can't blame you, though. It must have been spectacular."

"It was terrific."

While his mother got herself a mug of coffee and joined them at the kitchen table, he told them all about it. Almost all, that is, of course.

"What an awful thing for that boy to do!" said Mrs. Tearle. "The police are all over town this morning, looking for him. It gives me the creeps to think that he's still missing. I hear they're even dragging the canal."

"You mean they think he might have drowned himself?" said Shirley, wide-eyed.

"Well, you can't tell what anybody may do when they're that crazy."

Roger thought about Hazy sitting twenty feet away in his sleeping bag, and felt a little crazy himself. He decided he had better change the subject.

"Well, fire or no fire, we still have eggs to deliver. Mom, I feel okay this morning, I can make it around our route all right."

"Not on your life, young man. I want you to stay put till noon, and then we'll see how you're doing. I'll take Shirley and Thumbs in the car. We're going to pick him up on the way."

Roger grumbled, but accepted the verdict, being careful not to betray the fact that this was just what he wanted. Get everybody out of the house. Before they left he went obediently to his room, supposedly to return to bed. The car was scarcely out of the driveway before he was leaping into his clothes.

Grabbing a mess kit and a small Thermos bottle off his closet shelf, he hurried down to the kitchen, picked up the special telephone, and buzzed the tree house. Hazy's scratchy voice answered.

"Everybody's gone," Roger told him. "I'll be right out with some breakfast for you."

"Okay. I like my eggs — "

"You'll get bread and butter. I haven't got time to cook anything," snapped Roger, and hung up. "Eggs! You'd think this was a hotel!"

Working fast, he buttered three slices of bread, hesitated, and then took time to spoon a big gob of grape jelly into one section of the mess kit's tin plate as a special treat. Next he filled the Thermos bottle with milk. With Shirley around, swilling the stuff all the time, an extra pint here and there would never be missed.

When Roger climbed up into the tree house, he found Hazy Milford sitting in the chair at the desk. He looked for all the world like someone waiting to be served his breakfast.

"Here you are," said Roger, plunking the Thermos and mess kit down in front of him. Hazy took the cover off the plate and looked pained.

"I always have bacon and eggs for breakfast," he said. "Every morning."

"Then you should have brought along your own short order cook," said Roger. In his best sardonic manner he added, "I hope you can make do with grape jelly, we didn't have any strawberry jam."

"How about red raspberry?" asked Hazy. "I always have red raspberry at home."

He was perfectly serious about it all. Obviously, where eating was concerned, Hays Milford was a creature of habit. With nothing much else to live for, he took good care of his comforts.

"Here you get grape," said Roger, "or nothing."

Sighing, Hazy took the top out of the Thermos, and recoiled.

"Milk? I hate milk!"

"Now, listen, Hazy — "

"Oh, I know." The fugitive sighed again. "Beggars can't be choosers, so I'll have to make the best of it. But milk! If I have to eat stuff like this, I'd be better off in jail."

"You may get there yet." Fighting off the urge to kick Hazy out of the tree house and go call the police, Inspector Tearle sat on a corner of the desk and folded his arms. He looked down at his unbidden guest severely. "Now, we've got to talk fast, because I haven't much time to work with, and every minute counts. While my mother and sister are gone, I want to go over and look around at the scene. I'll have to keep an eye peeled for them as it is, because they'll be stopping at your house with eggs in half an hour or so."

Hazy was managing to stuff down a slice of bread, and was even beginning to eye the grape jelly with grudging interest.

"Have you thought of anything else about Fidel that might be of any help?" asked Roger.

Chewing monstrously, Hazy frowned and shook his head.

"Naugh." From his full mouth came a throttled sound evidently mean to be negative. He gulped like a pelican swallowing a fish whole, and then spoke more clearly. "No, I haven't. He isn't a guy you get to know much about."

"I guess not. Well, anyway, I'll go over and take a look around, and maybe I'll run onto something. Ought to be possible by now to really see anything that's left from the fire."

"Good luck," said Hazy, as coolly as though it were Roger who was in trouble instead of himself. "Listen, it's boring sitting out here alone with nothing to do. You got a portable radio I could borrow?"

Roger groaned.

"For crying out loud, Hazy! Don't you know the police are all over town, looking for you? You want them to drive by and hear music coming out of my tree house, and get ideas? I'll bring you a couple of books."

"Oh, all right. Got anything about cars?"

"I'll see."

"One more thing," said Hazy. "I have to go to the bathroom."

Inspector Tearle slumped down on the desk again. It began to seem to him as if more obstacles were being thrown in his path than any self-respecting detective could be expected to take.

"Oh, boy! That does it!"

Hazy laughed his painful, soundless laugh.

"Well, I'm only human."

"Are you sure?" asked Roger bitterly. "Well, let me take a look around. It's lucky not many people can see into our back yard. If nobody's around, you can come into the house. Wait a minute, I'll give you the word."

Roger climbed down and checked. Their house was on a corner, with only three other houses anywhere near it. None of their neighbors was in sight, and the streets were quiet.

"Okay," he said quietly, "come on!"

Hazy climbed down the ladder as unhurriedly as if he had not a care in the world, and strolled across the yard to the back door.

"Looks better if I don't run, if anyone's watching," he said, and this time Roger had to admire his coolness, if not his reasoning.

"Yes, but everybody knows you're missing. Even if

they didn't know you by sight, they might get ideas if they saw you. So don't overdo it."

Inside, Roger pointed the way to the bathroom. Hazy stopped beside a stack of magazines on the kitchen counter, and selected one.

"Now what are you doing?"

"I always read — "

"Not this time you don't!" snarled Roger, snatching the magazine away from him. "You get in there and make it snappy!"

"Oh, I'm tired of hiding!" said Hazy. "If I have to give up everything I like to do, what's the point of it? For two cents I'd turn myself in."

Roger glared at him. He was almost speechless — though, being Roger, not quite.

"Now, listen, you're not going to do any such thing! Why, if you gave up now, how would I look? I'd be in almost as big a jam as you are!"

It was a bad slip on the part of Inspector Tearle. Hazy's eyes widened, and then narrowed foxily. This time his laughter was almost audible.

"Say, that's right! You're really on the hook now, aren't you? Gee, maybe they'd even make us cell-mates!"

And still laughing, Hazy Milford picked up another magazine and disappeared into the bathroom, while Inspector Tearle folded up into a chair at the kitchen table and put his head in his hands.

There was no question about it. He had delivered himself into the hands of a monster. He had thought this might prove to be Inspector Tearle's Greatest Case. Instead, it was beginning to look like Inspector Tearle's Worst Case, if not indeed Inspector Tearle's Last Case. Hazy Milford, he reflected unhappily, was not the only one who was up a tree.

The Inspector's meditations were interrupted at this point by the squeal of brakes outside. His head came up, his eyes went to the window.

East Widmarsh's one and only police car had pulled up on the other side of the street. Constable Stubbert, looking red-eyed from lack of sleep and short-tempered from lack of success, was at the wheel, staring sideways.

He was staring at the tree house.

8

FOR THE SPACE of two or three seconds, Inspector
Tearle's machine-tooled brain refused to function.
His thoughts shattered into something resembling a
view through a kaleidoscope.

But then the discipline of twelve years reasserted
itself, and he knew what he had to do. Stumbling
onto feet that felt as though both had gone to sleep,
he walked out into the back yard toward the tree
house. Along the way he pretended to become aware
of the police car. He waved a friendly greeting to
his rival.

"Hi, Constable."

East Widmarsh's official guardian of the law returned the greeting in a perfunctory manner.

"Roger, why don't you get in bed and stay there?

Them eyes of yours still look like two burned holes in a blanket."

"Oh, I'm fine, Constable. I just *look* unhealthy," quipped Roger, continuing his steady way toward the tree house. Meanwhile, Constable Stubbert was climbing ponderously out of the police car. A square-built, middle-aged man, he was not at his best when maneuvering his paunch out from under a steering wheel.

"That Milford kid is still missing," he announced. "We haven't found him yet."

"That so? Gee, that's too bad."

"Don't tell me *you* haven't found him yet, either?" said the officer with exaggerated surprise. "You're so good at finding things, I figured by now you'd have him all located."

It was obvious that the Grimshaw Campstool Case and the McDermott Small Child Case, two of Inspector Tearle's earlier triumphs, were still rankling in the bosom of Constable Stubbert. But then he drew solace from a more recent case.

"Of course, you never had much luck with Chadburn's geese, but that's neither here nor there," he added with misplaced satisfaction. Little did he know, nor was he ever likely to know, how successful Inspector Tearle had been in that instance.

Roger paused at the foot of the ladder.

"Listen, that crazy kid is in my class at school,

and I'd hate to think where he might be right now," he declared with feeling.

"Well, he's got to be around here somewhere." Constable Stubbert's bloodshot eyes roamed upward again. "I was thinking just now, wouldn't it be funny if he'd holed up in your tree house?"

Inspector Tearle tried to acknowledge how funny this whimsical idea was with an appreciative laugh, but it was a pathetically dry sound that emerged, dry because it came from a dry throat.

"That would have been one for the books, all right," he agreed, "but I'm afraid we're out of luck. I've already been up there to get today's egg route list. But say, while you're here, how about coming up for a look, Constable? You've never seen my office. Come on!" urged Roger, and mounted the ladder. Would he have time to get the mess kit, the Thermos bottle, and the sleeping bag out of sight?

As Roger climbed inside, Constable Stubbert followed him to the foot of the ladder.

"Don't mind if I do," he said. "I've always wondered what you have up there in your famous office."

All great detectives depend on inspiration in times of peril. And now inspiration came to the aid of Inspector Tearle. He put his head out to look down at the constable.

"Watch out for splinters," he warned. "My father

got one in his foot just the other day when *he* came up."

"Splinters?" said Constable Stubbert, and was injudicious enough to run his finger across one of the rungs by way of testing for splinters. "Ow!"

"What's the matter?" cried Inspector Tearle hopefully.

"I got one, that's what!"

"Gee, I'm sorry, Constable. Wait, I'll come down and take it out for you!"

"Not on your life! I'll have it tended to at Town Hall!" snapped the injured man. "I should have known better than to fool around with — with — "

And he stamped back to his car, muttering remarks that Inspector Tearle could not catch, which was perhaps just as well. Up in the tree house, had he cared to listen, the constable might have heard a sigh of relief of large proportions.

As soon as the police car had disappeared down the street, Roger descended and hurried into the house.

"Okay, Hazy, either come out of there and get back in the tree house, or I'm turning you in personally, and I mean it!" he shouted. Inspector Tearle had had enough.

Almost at once Hazy obliged him, and this time he was enjoying himself so much that his laughter could have been heard for several feet around.

"I had a box seat for that whole bit," he declared, "and it was great! Roger, you're sensational! From now on, I'll do anything you want."

Roger simmered down a little, thankful for any improvement in the fugitive's attitude.

"Well, that's more like it!"

"Still, it's a lucky thing I *was* in here."

"Yes, maybe so, but the point is, you're holding up my investigation, and we haven't got a minute to waste. So get out there and stay there till I come back!"

"Got any oranges?" asked Hazy. "I always have orange juice — "

"Oh, for — Here!" Opening the refrigerator, Roger handed Hazy a couple of oranges. "Now wait a minute, until I make sure the coast is clear . . ."

At last Inspector Tearle was on his way to the scene of the crime.

As he trotted across the back fields and through the woods toward Fieldcrest, he worried. Never in his life had he been up against a case that was so disorganized and disheartening as this one. Never, certainly, had he been so uncomfortably involved personally. The search for Hazy was bound to intensify rapidly. Roger could not hope to keep him concealed for long, and unless he could prove Hazy innocent in fairly short order, he would be in terrible trouble himself. What if Hazy actually was lying? What if he really was the one who had set the fire? The mere possibility was enough to make Roger's stomach tighten up uneasily. Did Hazy Milford have him fooled? It was always there, that possibility.

When he reached the edge of the Fieldcrest grounds, Roger slowed down to a walk and watched ahead warily, making sure his family station wagon was not in the drive, nor anywhere in sight on the road. A couple of firemen and one small truck were still on hand, and two other men seemed to be inspecting the ruins and talking to Martin the chauffeur. Fidel was not in sight anywhere.

None of the men paid any attention to Roger. He was able to look around and listen without being bothered. One of the men had a camera slung over his shoulder, and was obviously a newspaper photographer. The other man seemed to be from the insurance company.

The two burned cars, half buried under water-soaked, blackened debris, were a melancholy sight. Only a few flecks of the green paint of the station wagon and the yellow paint of the Stutz Bearcat had survived on the twisted frames. Remembering how the Stutz had gleamed in the sunlight the day it was being loaded into the van, Roger grieved all over again for the fine old car. Still, he did not waste time contemplating that part of the wreckage, however sad, because he had more important things to do and needed to make every moment count. He moved on to the far end of the garage where Fidel's storeroom had been located.

"Yes, we've been in contact with Mr. Milford, and he's flying home today," Roger heard Martin tell the photographer. "He's concerned about the boy being missing."

Roger craned his neck this way and that to get the best possible view of the storeroom area. He wished he could have waded straight in among the ashes for a thoroughly good look, but knew he would be warned off if he tried it. His flesh crawled as he remembered his and Hazy's talk about the possibility of finding a body in the ruins, but nothing resembling a grisly pile of bones was visible. A small section of a partition was still standing, part of what must have been the wall between the storeroom and the Stutz's stall. And it looked as if there might have been a door in the wall. An inner door! It was the first exciting discovery he had made, the first one to set his mind racing.

He walked over where the men were standing. The insurance man, who was carrying a clipboard, was putting his pen away in his pocket.

"Well, I think I've got everything I need for now," he told Martin.

"If I can be of any more help, just let me know," said the chauffeur.

When the insurance man had walked away to his car, Martin noticed Roger, and nodded to him.

"Hi, Roger." Martin grinned at the reporter, and jerked his head at Roger. "This is the Inspector, as we call him here in East Widmarsh. He's our local detective. If you want to know anything about this business — how the fire started, where the boy disappeared to, anything — just ask the Inspector."

"That so? Glad to know you, Inspector, I'm Gary Stover," said the photographer, and mentioned the big national press association he worked for. Bald, and with a smooth round face, Stover looked bland and easy-going, and not too alert, until one noticed his shrewd, busy eyes. When they flicked his way, Roger knew he was being sized up expertly by someone who missed few details. Stover winked at Martin.

"Maybe I ought to interview the Inspector, at that," he said.

"I can't tell you much, Mr. Stover," said Roger. "I just wanted to ask Martin a question. Was there a door between the storeroom and the Stutz's stall?"

"A door? Why, yes, there was, Inspector."

"Was it locked?"

"You bet it was. Fidel always kept the doors of that storeroom of his locked tight. You'd have thought he had a — well, I don't know what — in there."

Roger tried not to look excited. If Fidel wanted to destroy the storeroom, wouldn't he set the fire in another part of the garage? If it had obviously started in the storeroom, then he might have been blamed for it, at least on the grounds of carelessness, especially when it was known that he kept the room so carefully locked that nobody else could have gotten in there. Of course, all of this involved a good deal of reasoning, but somehow Roger was convinced that Fidel was no fool.

"But now, wait a minute, Roger," said Martin, staring at him. "What are you getting at?"

"Nothing," said Roger. "I was just wondering."

"Sure. Just wondering." Martin rubbed his lean, handsome jaw thoughtfully. "Well, now you've got me wondering, too. You know, it's hard for me to believe that Hazy set that fire, no matter what they say . . . But don't quote me!" he added, with a glance at Gary Stover, who was looking interested.

Roger had been so intent on their conversation that he had forgotten to keep an eye on the road. Now he remembered to check it. It was well he did. He got one of those breaks that even the best detective needs now and then. He caught a flash of light blue through the trees, moving along the road.

"Oh, gosh, here comes Mom! Don't tell them you saw me, I'm supposed to be home in bed!" cried Roger, and turned to sprint for the woods. He covered the twenty-five yards of lawn between the garage and the woods at a clip that would have made an antelope stare in disbelief, and slid into tall grass like a ballplayer sliding into third base. He was out of sight by the time the station wagon rolled up the drive.

Peering out through the tall grass like an Indian scout watching an Apache war party, Roger saw his mother, Shirley, and Thumbs all step out of the car to have a look at the wreckage of the fire. Shirley was carrying a couple of cartons of eggs. After she had looked at the garage, she walked to the house to deliver them.

A moment later they were on their way again. Roger was breathing easier, and about to rise, when suddenly he froze. Someone was standing beside him, someone who had appeared without a sound. Roger's popeyed gaze traveled up a stained pair of rough trousers to a powerful pair of shoulders and on to a dark face as hard as a granite idol's, from which beady brown eyes looked down into his.

"Why you hide?" asked Fidel.

9

WHEN HE REPLIED, Roger's voice was so squeaky and scratchy that it must have reminded Fidel of Hazy's.

"I — I'm not supposed to be here. I mean, I'm supposed to be home in bed," stammered Roger, wishing for once that he was. With the covers pulled over his head. "My mother and my sister came to deliver eggs, and I didn't want them to see me."

The expression on Fidel's impassive face gave no indication as to whether he believed Roger or not, or what he thought about anything. He grunted, but even the grunt could have been taken in any of a dozen ways. Then he turned and walked off as abruptly as he had done the night of the fire, after they had finished with their bucket brigade.

For a moment Roger was still too paralyzed to

move. Then, when feeling gradually returned to his body, he scrambled to his feet. What did Fidel really think about him? Had he been around somewhere near enough to hear Roger talking to Martin? The very thought sent a new chill through his veins.

He would have liked to go back and look around some more, but with Fidel on the scene, and after what had just happened, it seemed a poor time to show special interest in the remains of the gardener's storeroom. No, he would go home and get back into his darned old pajamas and back in that darned old bed, so that when she came home his mother would find him there, and see that he was all right, and let him get up. Then he could think about coming back over to Fieldcrest.

He trotted home with more than enough problems on his mind to occupy him all the way. First of all, what about Shirley and Thumbs? He could not go much further without taking them into his confidence. Shirley would be deviling him to know what the surprise was he had hidden in the tree house. Besides, he would need their help. Then, what about his mother? Today was Friday. Fortunately on Fridays she had a bridge foursome. They had lunch and played cards all afternoon. So that was a break. He could deal with Hazy undisturbed, and there was plenty to do.

For one thing, he wanted no more moments like the one when Constable Stubbert nearly came up into the tree house. What if Hazy had been there? The first thing Roger meant to do was rig up some kind of hiding place that Hazy could get into in a pinch. Luckily the fugitive was so small it could be managed somehow.

With such thoughts and plans buzzing through his mind, Roger was almost surprised to look up and find himself home. Before leaving, he had put the ladder back in the garage, just to be on the safe side. Everything seemed to be all right, except that one of the tarps was rolled partway up. Roger brought out the ladder, set it into place, and climbed up to check on his client.

Seated on the folded sleeping bag, Hazy looked up from a book.

"What's the idea of fooling with the tarp?" demanded Roger.

"The light was rotten. I never read in a bad light," said Hazy. "Anyway, what's the difference? Anybody would think you left it up to air out the joint."

"Not if the wrong person happened to see you roll it up."

"I was careful. Gee, all you do is complain."

"*I* complain? That's good, that is!"

"Well, anyway, what did you find out? Anything?"

"Maybe. I don't know. Listen, I've got to go hop into bed, they'll be back before long. I just wanted you to know what's up. My mother will be going out to lunch soon. She'll be gone all afternoon. We can talk more then, and I'll tell you about my plans, and what happened. And I'm going to tell my sister and Thumbs Thorndyke about you, because I'll need their help. But don't worry about them."

Hazy's small, pinched face brightened up.

"Oh, that's okay. Let's *all* have a talk. It'll break the monotony."

"We will. We'll bring you some lunch. And don't tell me what you want, because you'll get whatever Shirley fixes."

"That'll be okay," said Hazy, looking unusually cooperative for a change.

"All right, then. We'll see you later."

Roger climbed down and put the ladder away again. He was getting tired of hauling it back and forth, but doing so was necessary. He reminded himself again that the rungs did need sanding. At the same time, he was glad he had not gotten around to sanding them as yet. He made up his mind not to do so until this present affair was out of the way.

When the egg deliverers returned home, they found him dutifully propped against his pillows in bed, with books and his chess correspondence around him. At the moment of their arrival he was examining the new magic trick he had sent for, the Swami's Card Box.

"Well! The patient is looking better. I knew a morning of extra rest would do you good," said his mother. "How do you feel?"

"I've had all the bed I can stand," said Roger. "Can I get up now?"

"Yes, I guess so. But I want you to take it easy for the rest of the day. Well, I've got to go change, if I'm going to get to lunch on time."

Mrs. Tearle had gone. Inspector Tearle and his assistants were alone, and Shirley was fixing her specialty for lunch. Tuna fish sandwiches. Roger was looking forward to the way Hazy would get told off when he made a face at her sandwiches. Just let him talk about how he always ate peanut butter and red raspberry jam, or something of the sort, and she would really pin his ears back!

Roger and Thumbs were sitting at the kitchen table, watching Shirley work, when she asked,

"What about your big surprise out in the tree house, the one you didn't want me to see yet?"

"Did you say anything about it to Mom?"

"No, because if I did I'd have to tell her about how you came out in your pajamas when you were supposed to be in bed."

"Good. Well . . ."

Roger was considering what was the best way to break the big news to them when an unexpected sound made them all jump.

The special telephone buzzed.

Shirley dropped her spreader and turned to stare.

"Hey! What's going on?" cried Thumbs.

"Take it easy," said Roger. He went to the phone and answered. "What's the big idea?"

Judging by the momentary silence that followed, Hazy was laughing.

"I just wanted to give you all a thrill," he squeaked.

"Well, you did. Now lay off. We'll be out with lunch in a minute."

Roger hung up and turned around to enjoy the general astonishment of two open mouths.

"I was just going to tell you," he said. "Make enough sandwiches for four. We have a guest for lunch."

"A guest? Who?"

Inspector Tearle was never one to avoid squeezing all the drama possible out of a given situation. There were times, in fact, when he was plainly and simply a ham. Now was one of those times. He allowed himself to walk back across the kitchen with all the outrageous aplomb of an aging character actor. Not until he had sat down again at the table did he deliver his bombshell.

"Hazy Milford," he said.

The ensuing uproar was all he could have asked for. Gratifying indeed.

"*Hazy M — Milford?*" stammered Shirley at the top of her lungs.

"*Hazy?* Oh, no!" wailed Thumbs in the voice of a

strong man near tears. He pulled himself together enough to ask the obvious question. "What's he doing in *our* tree house?"

"It's a long story. I might as well start at the beginning," said Inspector Tearle, sure of his audience. "Keep working on those sandwiches, Shirl — I'm getting hungry, and I'm sure that little creep out there is too."

While Shirley made sandwich after sandwich, scarcely conscious of what she was doing, Roger told them everything.

"And to think we were fooling around over there at that silly old carnival!" said Shirley, so thoroughly put out that she forgot entirely how much fun she had had there.

"What I can't understand is, how could you believe anything that little wart said!" complained Thumbs. "I'd have turned him in so fast — "

"No, you wouldn't have," said Roger, well aware of his friend's just and generous nature. "If you'd been here, you'd have done exactly what I did."

"Like fun I would!" said Thumbs, but without much conviction.

"Yes, you would. But anyway, now I'm on the hook. You can see that. I've got to prove that Fidel did it, and Hazy didn't, or *I'm* in big trouble, too. And right now, if anything goes wrong, I want you both to understand one thing. You didn't know anything about this."

"Why not?"

Inspector Tearle sighed in the face of such innocence.

"Why not? Because if Hazy *is* guilty I'll be an accessory after the fact, that's what! And I don't want you to be one too, either of you."

"What's an accessory after the fact?" asked Shirley. She sounded as if she suspected it of involving some form of disease, like leprosy.

"An accessory after the fact is someone who helps a criminal after the criminal has committed a crime, while knowing full well that the criminal *did* commit the crime," explained Roger, who had not read hundreds of mystery stories for nothing. Furthermore, before getting back into bed he had taken the trouble to look up the subject in the encyclopedia, so now he was able to add what he had learned there, reeling it off from memory. "An accessory after the fact is one who, knowing a man has committed a felony, receives, harbors, or assists him — and I'm doing all three. Accessories after the fact are in general punishable with imprisonment, with or without hard labor, for a period not exceeding two years."

Shirley stared at him for a moment.

"Oh," she said.

Thumbs gaped at Shirley, then at Roger.

"Oh," said Thumbs.

"Well, anyway, just remember, both of you. If anything goes wrong, you didn't know a thing about what was going on."

Thumbs thought this over, and didn't like it.

"The heck with that," he said. "If you go to jail for not exceeding two years, so do I."

Inspector Tearle sprang to his feet to conceal the warm feeling his knuckleheaded friend's devotion had aroused in him.

"Oh, for Pete's sake. I don't *want* you to . . . to . . ."

He took a turn up and down the kitchen, looking like a worried crane on his long skinny legs, and then grinned his sad-eyed grin at them.

"Well, we'll just have to find out who did it, and then *none* of us will go to jail — except whoever did it."

The phone buzzed again. Roger rolled his eyes, and went to answer.

"Room service," he announced wearily. "What is it now? . . . Oh. Well, okay, wait a minute till I come out and see if it's safe."

Roger hung up and explained.

"He wants to come in and wash up for lunch."

"It fits," said Thumbs scornfully.

Roger went outside for a look around, and made one more trip with the ladder.

"Okay, come ahead."

Hazy climbed down, and they hurried into the house. Shirley stared at him as he entered, showing more interest in the small, unattractive boy than she ever had before. Thumbs glowered at him disapprovingly. Hazy treated them to one of his foxy grins.

"Bet you're surprised to see me!"

"That's not the half of it!" growled Thumbs.

Hazy went on through the house to the bathroom. Roger turned to the others.

"Okay, let's take the food out to the tree house. Hazy can sit on the floor out of sight. You take the sandwiches, Shirl. Thumbs, you bring the milk, and don't drop it, and I'll bring the mugs."

"But you don't like milk," Shirley pointed out.

"Today I'll make do," said Roger, suppressing a smile that threatened to be downright sadistic. "You two go ahead. I'll wait for Hazy."

After some little time the fugitive appeared. Roger gave him a nettled look. Not only had Hazy spruced up his clothes as best he could, but Roger could have sworn he had even combed his hair.

"You pick a fine time to primp," he snapped. "Come on, let's get moving!"

When they joined the others in the tree house, the tarps were all rolled up, the sandwiches were in four piles on paper napkins on the desk, and a large bottle of milk was standing beside them.

"Sit down on the floor," ordered Roger, "so you'll be out of sight."

Hazy sat down on the sleeping bag. Shirley handed him a sandwich.

"Here," she said. "It's tuna fish."

"Thank you!' said Hazy, eyeing his sandwich with every evidence of pleasure. While Shirley was pouring milk, he bit into it, chewed, and swallowed. "Say, this is delicious! How do you make them like this?"

Shirley looked surprised at his question. At the same time, no one could have said that she looked annoyed, or even impatient.

"Oh. I mix up the tuna fish with some mayonnaise, and put in some salt and pepper," she said.

"Well, I wish you'd teach our cook to make them like this," said Hazy. "Hers can't touch yours."

"Well, I — well, thanks," said Shirley, scarcely knowing how to react to such enthusiasm. Roger and Thumbs had never said anything about her sandwiches, one way or the other. They merely wolfed them down every time she made them.

She handed Hazy a mug of milk.

"Oh, thank you!" he said, for all the world as though she had given him a bottle of red raspberry soda pop, or whatever it was he always drank at home. This was too much for Roger.

"Hey, what is this? You hate milk!"

"That depends," said Hazy. "Depends on who's handing it out." As he grinned at Roger, his sallow face reddened. "After all, you're not the . . . the prettiest girl in school."

❀ 10

IF THE STOUT OLD OAK TREE had been shaken to the roots, and had thrown their tree house to the ground, Roger and Thumbs could not have been jolted much harder. Shirley was a twin sister, an Amazon, a tomboy they had to put up with. They were completely unprepared for the idea that someone had taken a good look at her. And to call her the prettiest girl in school!

"Listen, you watch what you say!" warned Thumbs in a choked voice.

Roger had glanced at Shirley, and was horrified by what he saw. Hazy's remark had brought some definitely feminine pink spots to her tanned cheeks — before they turned bright red altogether. Instead of belting Hazy one as Roger would have expected, she just sat there looking stunned. Roger was appalled. This little monster's bad manners knew no bounds! It was the most embarrassing moment he could remember, and he hastened to bring matters back under control.

"Now, look, you shut up and eat!" he ordered harshly and unnecessarily, for Hazy had been overcome by an attack of shyness the instant the fatal words were out, and seemed now to be trying to hide his own red face behind his sandwich. "We haven't got time for any — any — For crying out loud, while we're sitting here eating tuna fish sandwiches, the police are even dragging the canal, and your father is flying back from Europe!"

Hazy paused in the middle of a bite.

"He is?"

"Yes. I heard Martin say so."

"Well, what do you know?" murmured Hazy.

With that, Roger told them all about his morning's activities. When he got to the part about the door between the storeroom and the Stutz's stall, Hazy nodded.

"That's right, there was a door there. One time when I was looking at the Stutz, I tried to open it, to see if I could sneak into Fidel's storeroom that way, but it was locked."

"Martin said Fidel always kept it locked. He said, 'You'd have thought he had a — well, I don't know what — in there.' That's just the way he said it. Then he looked funny and said, wait a minute, what was I getting at, and I said, nothing, I was just wondering. And then he said, now I had him wondering about Fidel, too."

"Good. Now he'll keep his eyes open, and watch Fidel, and maybe *he'll* come up with something."

"I hope so. I'll say one thing for Martin, he sort of stuck up for you. He said it was hard for him to believe you started the fire, no matter what they said."

"He did?" The scratchy sound of Hazy's voice seemed more cynical than ever. "That's more than I would have expected from him."

"Why? Doesn't he like you?"

"No, not really," said Hazy in a way that made Roger realize just how bleak his life was. Hazy did not have a single friend, not one person he was sure liked him. The boy shrugged. "But then Martin doesn't care much about anybody except himself. He's out for Number One."

"But he doesn't dislike you enough to want to start a fire just to get you into trouble, does he?"

"Martin? No, that's not his style. He couldn't be bothered to hate me that much. I may have pulled a few tricks on him, but nothing he'd want to get back at me for. Besides, one thing he *does* like besides himself is cars. He liked that old Stutz as much as I did myself. I don't think he could have stood to burn it up, any more than I could have. Anyway, do you know how much that car was worth?"

He glanced around the group for an answer.

"A couple of thousand dollars?" ventured Thumbs. Hazy snickered.

"A couple of thousand? Just ten times that much, is all!"

"What? Twenty thousand dollars?"

"That's right. Maybe even more."

"Twenty thousand! For an old car!" Thumbs whistled, still finding it hard to believe.

"An *antique* car," corrected Hazy. "The kind I'm talking about is an old car that's been put back into perfect shape, like ours was. You can get old cars in bad condition for a couple of thousand, maybe, but

putting them into shape is liable to cost you ten thousand more. My dad spent more than that on ours, and it was one of the best Stutz Bearcats in the whole country. No. Martin wouldn't burn up a car like *that*, not even if he hated me like poison!"

"Okay, I'm convinced," said Roger. Next he told about hiding when he saw his family station wagon coming.

"What? You were right there?" said Shirley. "I wish I'd known!"

"I'm glad you didn't," said Roger. Then he described the way Fidel had suddenly appeared beside him.

"I'll bet you nearly passed out!" said Thumbs.

"I sure did. I don't mind saying he scared me stiff. I just hope he hadn't heard me talking to Martin."

"You're lucky he didn't cut your throat," said Hazy cheerfully.

"I wouldn't want to be around him again on a dark night," admitted Roger.

"Well, now, what are we going to do?" asked Thumbs.

The thoughtful expression that creased Inspector Tearle's brow showed that his mind had not been idle.

"We've got to go over there and look around some more, and I think we'll have to get Martin to help us. He could go in and really take a good look through the ashes in Fidel's storeroom, and maybe turn up some clues. Then he could tip off the police or do some investigating of Fidel. If Fidel goes anywhere, he ought to be followed. If only we knew who those men were who came to see him and went in the store-room with him, and what it was they took away with them!"

Roger paused and had Hazy tell the others what he had seen the night he watched Fidel and his visitors.

"The only trouble is, we can't tell Martin about *them*," said Roger.

"Why not?" asked Shirley.

"Can't you see? How could we possibly know any-thing about them, if Hazy hadn't told us? And we can't very well tell Martin that Hazy told us!"

"Oh, that's so."

"Well, then. We're really in a tough spot. But if we can only just turn up something — anything — we'll have a start. And we'd better get going. Oh, but first, I want to fix up a hiding place for Hazy," added Roger, and told them about Constable Stubbert's visit. The part about the splinter got a big laugh. Then Thumbs asked,

"But how can we hide Hazy up here?"

"You know that big pasteboard carton in the garage? It'll go under the desk, and it's big enough for him to get into if he has to. Let's bring it up."

The carton worked out fine. When Hazy crawled in one end and sat doubled up inside it, he was com-pletely concealed.

"Okay. That's just in case," said Roger. "Now let's get going."

"I wish I could go too," said Hazy. "I hate it here, just sitting around."

"Never mind that, stay down out of sight, and keep quiet."

"I will. Thanks for the lunch, Shirley."

"Oh, that's all right," said Shirley, growing pink-cheeked again, while Roger and Thumbs exchanged a disgusted glance.

They were carrying their milk mugs and the milk bottle back to the house when the value of Inspector Tearle's foresight received prompt and spectacular proof. A car came around the corner and stopped. Gary Stover stepped out with his camera hanging from his shoulder. He waved to Roger, and stood looking up at the tree house with an appreciative grin on his round face.

"Hi. That chauffeur over at Fieldcrest told me about your office, Inspector," he said. "I thought I'd come over and take a few pictures. Might make a good Sunday feature. Would you kids mind posing?"

11

STOVER LOOKED from one strained face to another, and laughed.

"Don't tell me you're scared of having your pictures taken?"

Inspector Tearle was often at his best in a tight spot. He rose to the occasion now. It was important to make Stover think he was right about why they looked so scared. Otherwise he might get ideas.

"But, gee, you mean our pictures will be in newspapers all over the country?" said Roger, as if the idea awed him.

"Oh, now, don't let that bother you," said Stover. "Just relax. We'll have fun!"

Roger turned to the others.

"Well, what do you say?"

Thumbs shrugged his shoulders, and Shirley nodded uncertainly.

"Well, okay," said Roger.

"Good! Can I use your phone for a minute first?" asked Stover.

"Sure. Come on," said Roger, glad of a chance to let Hazy crawl inside his box and get settled. They all went into the house, and the reporter made a collect call to his office in New York City.

"Just had to report in," he said, when he had finished. His sharp eyes took note of the extra phone in the kitchen. "What's that, a homemade extension?"

"No, that's a private line to my office," said Roger. "Stay here, I'll give you a call."

Leaving Stover beside the telephone, Roger rushed out and climbed up into the tree house. Hazy was not in sight. Roger tapped on the carton.

"You okay in there?"

Hazy answered by tapping back.

"I'm okay for a while," he added in a muffled voice, "but get rid of him as fast as you can. It's no picnic being in here."

"I know, but you've got to be careful. One little sound from you, and we've had it," said Roger worriedly. He picked up the phone receiver and buzzed the kitchen. Stover answered, and talked for a minute, joking and enjoying himself.

"Well, we'll come on out and shoot some pictures now, okay, Inspector?"

"Come ahead," said Inspector Tearle.

Gary Stover was thorough. He took pictures of the tree house from several angles, with Roger and Shirley and Thumbs hanging out of the windows. He snapped them climbing the ladder, and standing in the doorway. When he climbed up for "a few interiors," as he called them, Roger wished a big splinter on him, but Stover managed not to pick up any. He took several more pictures, mostly of the Inspector sitting at his desk with the steel file in the background. Stover stood on the ladder to take these pictures, and it seemed to Roger as if he would never finish fiddling with his camera, adjusting this and changing that. To sit at the desk and try to look relaxed with a time bomb beside his feet was one of the stiffest challenges Inspector Tearle had ever been called upon to meet. All Hazy had to do was sneeze, or get a cramp and have to move, and it was all over.

"Well, that ought to do it," Stover said at last, after what seemed like at least the hundredth picture. He climbed down the ladder, thanked them, made sure he had all their names right, and drove away. They waited till the car disappeared around the corner. Then they rolled in the grass, whooping with relief. Scuffling sounds up in the tree house indicated that Hazy was coming out of his hiding place. He crawled into sight on his hands and knees and peered down at them. His flushed face showed that his ordeal had not been an easy one. He collapsed in the doorway, panting as though he badly needed a breath of fresh air.

"Let's not have any more visitors!" he squeaked. "I couldn't stand much more of that."

"Poor Hazy!" said Shirley. "I don't see how you did it!"

Thumbs groaned aloud, and Roger inwardly. Next she'd be making a hero out of the little monkey!

"Boy! What you put me through, Roger, is really something," said Hazy.

"What *I* put *you* through? I wish you'd remember, Hazy, none of this was my idea!" snapped Roger. "Stay out of sight, now, and we'll go over to your place and see what we can find out."

Roger had been counting heavily on Martin's help in their investigations. When they reached Fieldcrest, the chauffeur was starting up the Bentley.

"Hi, Martin. We want to look around, and I'd like to talk to you about some ideas we have," said Roger.

"I can't talk now, Inspector, I've got to drive to the airport and pick up Mr. Milford," said Martin. "You go ahead and look around, and when I get back we can have a talk."

Exasperated, Inspector Tearle watched the Bentley roll away down the drive. That pest of a photographer had delayed them just long enough to spoil his plans. Hang-ups like this were especially disheartening when time was so important. The strain of keeping

Hazy hidden was beginning to tell on Roger's nerves.

He took a look around.

"Well, at least I don't see Fidel anywhere. Thumbs, go check the side lawn. Shirl, see if maybe he's out in front, working on the flower beds or something."

While his assistants ran off on their errands, Inspector Tearle walked over to the garage for another look at the storeroom area. He was studying the ashes, longing to wade into them for a closer inspection, when the others returned.

"We didn't see him anywhere."

"Okay. Then I'd better grab my chance," said Roger, and crunched over ashes and debris into the center of the burned-out storeroom.

He had hardly done so when sounds of a door opening startled them all.

"Hey! Here he comes out of his house!" warned Thumbs in a low voice.

Roger scrambled hastily out of the ashes, but Fidel was already coming toward them. His dark eyes glittered under a heavy frown.

"You kids! Stay away," he said, waving them back.

"Okay, Fidel. We were just looking," said Roger.

"You go!" said Fidel, looking angrier than Roger had ever seen him.

"Sure! Come on," said Roger, and led an ignominious retreat in the direction of the path back to his own house. The others followed him silently until they reached the woods.

"Well, *that* sure was a big nothing!" Shirley summed it up.

Roger stopped and sat down on a big rock beside the path. He shook his head gloomily.

"We just can't seem to get a break. Now I've really done it, as far as putting Fidel on his guard goes. If he's not suspicious about what we're up to by now, he's dumber than I think he is. For that matter, it didn't feel right when I *was* in his storeroom. I just had the feeling I was on the wrong track, somehow, but I don't know what else we can do."

Shirley and Thumbs exchanged a glance of deep concern. Never had they seen their leader look so so close to total defeat. The limitations he had to work under, with no authority to press an investigation, began to seem insurmountable. Shoulders bowed, his sad eyes at their saddest, he got to his feet again.

"Come on," he said. "We might as well go home."

The setting he found himself in, a balmy summer's day, seemed like calculated mockery. It affronted his present mood, which called for winter's chill, and a deep snow in which to leave bloody footprints reminiscent of Valley Forge. Such was Inspector Tearle's state of mind, and it was not improved when, as they walked across the fields, a State Police car came along the street in front of their house. They watched uneasily while it went on past and out of sight again.

"I'll bet they've got a dozen cars snooping around

by now," said Roger. "And wait till Mr. Milford gets home. He'll probably turn out the National Guard for a house-to-house search."

Hazy peeped out at them when they walked into the yard.

"Back so soon?"

Roger gave him a brief report.

"So my father really did come back," said Hazy, his foxy face twisted into a strange smile. "Well, you can bet he'll really make the fur fly."

"I expect so. I'm going inside for a minute," said Roger, and walked away abruptly to the house. He wanted to be alone for a while and do some heavy thinking, because thinking was the only thing left to him. Toiling up the stairs, he sought his own room, and flung himself down on his bed with a groan of pure frustration. Actually, he didn't feel too well. Maybe he hadn't got rid of his bug after all.

For a few moments he stared at the ceiling, his mind an unaccustomed blank. Was this the end of the line for the Firebug Case? His eyes strayed wearily to his worktable, idly noting the objects that cluttered it. A pile of mail that needed answering. A table lamp he was going to rewire for his mother. A paperback book about the wonders of biochemistry, a field he thought might eventually interest him as a scientist. The small shipping carton containing the Swami's Card Box.

As his eyes rested on the carton, a green light seemed to flicker feebly somewhere in the depths of his mind. It was a signal he could not catch, but a signal nonetheless, and Inspector Tearle knew better than to disregard such flashes, however slight they might be. The Swami's Card Box was trying to tell him something, so to speak — but what?

Pulling himself slowly to his feet — he really felt quite seedy and used up — he slouched to his table and slumped into his chair, staring at the carton. Opening it, he pulled out the Swami's Card Box and stared at *it* for a while, waiting and hoping for a sudden blinding flash of understanding. But nothing

happened. The round box, with its dome-shaped cover, ornamented with exotic symbols suggestive of the Mysterious East, squatted on the table in front of him, an enigma. Almost angrily he snatched it up along with its carton and marched downstairs.

Thumbs and Shirley were in the kitchen, having a glass of milk and some cookies. Shirley was on the phone, talking to Hazy.

"You're sure you don't want some more milk? . . . Well, okay, I'll bring you some cookies when we come out."

"Ha! I'll bet he doesn't want any more milk, the little faker!" said Roger, as she hung up. He set the Swami's Card Box down on the table. "Okay, we're going to have a magic show."

They stared at him in amazement.

"Roger, this is no time to be doing silly card tricks!" said Shirley. "Are you sick again, or something? You look awful pale."

"I'm fine," said Roger grimly, "and I know what I'm doing. There's something about this box that almost gave me an idea, but I can't quite get hold of it. Maybe if I do the trick, whatever it is will come to me."

From the carton he produced a scarf and a wand, and laid them aside on the table.

"I really ought to put on my magician's turban, but we haven't got time for that," he muttered, as he took out a deck of cards. He fanned out the deck expertly and thrust it at Thumbs. "Here, take a card, any card."

Thumbs took a card. It was the seven of hearts.

"Okay. Now, tear it in two."

"You mean it?"

"Yes! Tear it in two."

"Well, okay," said Thumbs, and obliged.

"Now put those pieces together and tear them in two."

Thumbs obeyed.

"Now, once more. Tear them all up."

Flourishing the wand over the box with one hand, Roger took the lid off it with the other. Inside was a small round tray.

"Put the pieces in the tray, and stir them around."

When Thumbs had done this, Roger made some more passes over them with the wand.

"Now, find one corner of the card, a piece with the number on it," he said, stirring the pieces with the end of the wand. "There's one — see it? Take it and keep it in your hand. Don't let it get away from you for a minute!"

It seemed, however, to be a time when nothing was destined to go right for Roger. Thumbs took the corner of the card in what he intended to be a death-grip, but being Thumbs he managed to fumble it and drop it on the floor. And being part of a magic trick, it seemed to have some magic of its own, because it promptly disappeared. With a snort of annoyance, Roger dropped to his knees and began looking for it, but it was nowhere to be seen.

"Darn it, what did you have to do that for?" he cried, thoroughly put out. There is nothing worse in the magician's world than having the rhythm of a good trick interrupted by a slip of that sort.

Meanwhile, Shirley was being helpful.

"Never mind," she said brightly, poking around in the pieces of torn-up card and finding what she was after. "Here's the other corner, with the number on it and everything."

On his hands and knees under the table, Roger lifted his head and bumped it severely. Furious now, he scrambled to his feet, rubbing the bump he had collected.

"Darn you, anyway, Shirl!" he snarled, beside himself with rage. "Why can't you keep your hands off things?"

Shirley blinked.

"What's the matter? What did I do? What's wrong with this corner? It's just as good as the one Thumbs dropped!"

Roger glared at her.

"Oh, for Pete's sake! If you must know, the point is, it's not . . . not . . ."

Suddenly Inspector Tearle was transfixed. He had

frozen into a statue that was staring into space. A new gleam had come into eyes that only a moment before had been filled with the petulant fury of one who was, among other things, a cranky semi-invalid who should have gone to bed. The color in his pale cheeks improved even as they watched. When at last he spoke again, his voice was vibrant.

"That's it!" he cried, and the impact of the truth almost caused him to stagger back a step. "That's got to be it!"

❦ *12*

Inspector Tearle dashed for the door.

"I've got to talk to Hazy!"

They hurried out after him, and saw him swarm up the tree house ladder like a pirate boarding a treasure ship. When they followed him, he was nose to nose with Hazy, asking him questions that didn't seem to make any sense at all.

"That's great! But can you remember the man's name?" he was saying after a while. "You've got to remember his name, and where he lives!"

"Sure I can remember. I've read his ads often enough," said Hazy, and supplied the information Roger was after.

"Gangway!" said Roger, springing to the ladder. "I've got to make a phone call!"

He paused long enough to add impressively,

"A long distance phone call!"

Then he was down the ladder and shooting back into the house like a rocket. But when he put his call through, his luck deserted him. The line was busy.

"Well, keep trying, operator, and call me back as soon as you reach the number, please!"

He was fidgeting in a chair beside the phone, waiting, when it seemed to him his luck had gone for good. Two cars swung around the corner and pulled up alongside the house. One was driven by Gary Stover. The other was driven by Constable Stubbert. While Roger's heart bounded into his throat, both men jumped out and hurried across the lawn, straight toward the tree house. Roger rushed to the back door and looked out. Somehow he managed to summon up a ghastly smile of welcome.

"Hi! Is something up?"

"Something sure is, Inspector," said Stover breezily, "and I think the Milford boy is up — there!"

He pointed to the tree house.

"Come on down, Hazy," he said. "Don't bother to crawl back in that carton."

To say that Inspector Tearle was not staggered would be an untruth. But even in defeat, his curiosity continued to function.

"How did you know?" he asked.

Stover was only too glad to tell him. His round face was aglow with self-satisfaction.

"After I left here, I finally got around to thinking about something I'd noticed. You kids were carrying some mugs you'd been using in the tree house. It suddenly occurred to me there were four of them. Then I began to see some other things in a different light. The way you all looked at me when I first showed up. That big carton up in your office. I put two and two together, and came up with Hazy Milford."

Never could it be said that Inspector Tearle was too small-spirited to appreciate an outstanding bit of deductive reasoning, even when it was at his own expense.

"That's darn good," he admitted. "Hazy, you might as well come down."

Constable Stubbert was standing by with the air of a man who had suddenly found himself at the end of a rainbow, complete with pot of gold. Or perhaps, considering the way he was eyeing Roger, it would be more accurate to say he resembled a cannibal looking at a pot with a missionary in it. He all but licked his lips.

For a moment, however, the constable forgot about Roger. They all forgot about everything else as Hazy Milford appeared in the doorway of the tree house.

"Hold it, Hazy!" cried Stover, busy with his camera. "One more! Okay, now, come down the ladder, but slowly. I want a couple more shots."

"Hazy Milford!" said Constable Stubbert, goggling at the boy. "Well, I'll be a . . ."

The constable never finished saying what he would be, but no doubt he was remembering how close he had come to discovering Hazy's hideout himself, earlier in the day, only to be tricked out of that triumph by his self-appointed competition. No doubt it was thoughts such as these that made his red-eyed gaze so vengeful as he turned it back toward Roger.

"Well, now, as for you, *Inspector*," he said, bearing down on the word with heavy-footed irony, "you've gone a little too far this time, my boy. Of course, I don't have to tell an expert like you what an accessory after the fact is . . ."

"No, I know."

"Okay, then, *Inspector*, that there is what I'm arresting you as. So come along — "

Behind Roger, the telephone rang. At the sound, every disk in his spine seemed to rattle together like castanets.

"There's the phone! I'll be with you in just a minute, Constable!" he cried, and raced through the house.

"Hello? Mr. Farraday? This is Roger Tearle. I'm calling from East Widmarsh, and I need some information very much!"

The kitchen screen door slammed. Determined footsteps clumped through the house.

"All right, now, Roger, you come here this minute!" ordered the majesty of the law. "What do you think you're — "

Roger covered the mouthpiece of the phone with his hand.

"Please, Constable! It's a long distance call!"

In the act of grabbing him by the collar, Constable Stubbert pulled up short, stopped by the magic words.

"Huh! Well, hurry up!" he fumed. But he waited, while Roger clung desperately to the phone, like a storm-tossed sailor to a lifeline, and continued his conversation.

"Do you remember his name? Well, that doesn't matter," said Roger, thinking that probably the man he had in mind had given a false name anyway. "What did he look like? . . . Good! And what about the man with him? . . . Great! And what about their . . . Yes! Can you describe it? . . . That's it! Thanks, Mr. Farraday, thanks a lot! I'll call you back later and explain!"

With a spasm of relief, Inspector Tearle set the phone receiver back in its cradle as tenderly as if it had been a baby, and turned to give himself up.

Constable Stubbert looked as if he were contemplating a little police brutality.

"What was all that supposed to be about?" he demanded. "You stop your stalling and come along, and be quick about it! Mr. Milford's probably home by now, and I want to be there when we wrap this case up!"

"Did Mr. Stover take Hazy and Shirley and Thumbs over to Fieldcrest?"

"Yes! So I want to get over there — "

"And get your share of the credit," said Roger, nodding understandingly. "I don't blame you, Constable. But how about doing *better* than that?"

Constable Stubbert stared at him with deep suspicion.

"What do you mean, better? Never mind any more of your tricks!"

"Listen, Constable," insisted Inspector Tearle, "how would you like to be a *real* hero?"

❧ 13

CONSTABLE STUBBERT climbed behind the wheel of his police car and glowered at his passenger.

"Roger, you'd better be right about this, or heaven help you! I ought to have my head examined, letting you talk me into calling the State Police and sending them off on a wild goose chase like that!"

"Constable, it's *got* to be right! And if they have a police car in the area, like they said, we ought to know for sure any minute."

"But I still can't believe . . . Oh, I tell you, I ought to have my head examined!" repeated Constable Stubbert, ramming his car into gear. With a few jerks and rumbles, they were on their way. When they turned into the driveway at Fieldcrest, they saw the Bentley parked in it.

"Mr. Milford's here, all right," said Roger, and had his door open before the car was fairly stopped. He raced toward the house, leaving the arresting officer to grunt his way out and hurry after him yelling, "Hi! Hold on there!"

In the east wing of the house there was a summer living room with a series of French windows that opened like doors onto the back lawn. Hazy was looking out from one of these.

"Here he comes!" he called into the room over his shoulder. His foxy grin was anxious but hopeful as he stepped back to let Roger enter, with the constable almost on his heels. The group inside included Mr. Milford, Gary Stover, Martin, Shirley, and Thumbs. Stover was sitting at a desk, dictating his story over the telephone to someone in his office. Mr. Milford was pacing back and forth, puffing fiercely on a big cigar. When he saw Roger, he stopped and squared around to face him with anything but a welcoming expression.

"Well! So you're the one he was hiding out with! I thought better of you, Roger. This boy of mine," he said, with a cold glance at Hazy, "this boy of mine refused to say anything till you got here. So you'd better have a good story, or . . ."

"I have, Mr. Milford."

The lord of the manor was not used to being interrupted, but the authoritative ring of Inspector Tearle's voice left him with his mouth open.

"I got to hang up now, the other kid's just come in," Stover was saying on the phone. "I'll get back to you in a few minutes."

He grinned across the room at Roger.

"Hi, Inspector. What you got up your sleeve now?"

Roger was meeting Mr. Milford's challenging stare unblinkingly.

"Mr. Milford, do you remember a Stutz Bearcat that was offered for sale in Caspertown, Pennsylvania, one that Hazy wanted you to buy for spare parts?"

The big man nodded impatiently.

"Certainly I remember. What's that got to do with anything? I checked up on it — "

"You did?" said Hazy. He looked both pleased and hurt. "You never told me you did."

"Don't interrupt," ordered his father. "I checked up on it, and found out it had been in an accident years ago. The engine was beyond repair, and the frame had been twisted. The owner had tried to fix it up, but for my money it wasn't worth anything."

"Not even a thousand dollars?" asked Roger.

"Not even that."

"Well, somebody else felt different. Somebody else — "

Behind Mr. Milford, the desk phone rang. Annoyed, he snatched up the receiver and barked into it.

"What is it? Oh — just a minute. Constable, it's for you."

Exchanging a swift glance with Roger, Constable Stubbert hurried to the phone. His conversation was brief, and when he turned around again he was struggling not to look too dumfounded.

"Well, Constable? Is it where we thought it was?" asked Roger.

His use of "we" was not lost on his ancient rival, nor unappreciated.

"Right, Inspector," said Constable Stubbert. "It was exactly where we thought it was."

Inspector Tearle turned back to Mr. Milford. If the sweep of his arm was somewhat dramatic, if it was reminiscent of his passes as an amateur magician, such theatrics were perhaps pardonable. He was about to make the most astounding announcement of his career.

"Your Stutz Bearcat is safe and sound, Mr. Milford, a couple of miles from Burgessville," he said, "in *his* father-in-law's barn!"

Over against the wall, Martin had turned the color of the woodwork, and the woodwork was oyster white.

Constable Stubbert had departed triumphantly with his new prisoner, to lodge him in the single cell that constituted the village jail in the town hall. Gary

Stover had taken a lot of new pictures. And now Inspector Tearle was reconstructing the case for a rapt audience.

"He knew you'd be gone when they brought the Stutz back from the repair shop, Mr. Milford. He took your Stutz from the shop to his father-in-law's farm, switched it for the one he'd bought, and brought that one here. He waited till he knew Hazy would have to be at the dentist's, so that Hazy wouldn't see the other car."

"It looked pretty good, that other car," said Mr. Milford, "but Hazy would have known in a minute it wasn't ours."

"That's right. So then, Martin offered to take Hazy to the carnival, and said they'd start at nine. He knew Hazy would be out by the garage, hanging around, waiting to go, when the fire started."

"Pretty slick. He buys himself a Stutz for a thousand, and trades it for mine," said Mr. Milford with a hard grin. "Then all he has to do is wait a while, quit his job here, take my Stutz out West somewhere, register it in another state, and sell it for twenty or twenty-five thousand. With a nice nest egg like that, he'd be in good shape. He must have thought he had a foolproof set-up, all right."

"Sure he did. He knew everybody would figure that Hazy started the fire."

Mr. Milford nodded.

"Including me," he admitted, with a shamefaced

glance at his son. "Hazy, maybe I'm the one that needs to go to military school."

For a long moment they looked at each other across the room. When Mr. Milford spoke again, his voice was softer and less certain of itself than Roger had ever heard it.

"I expect we can get someone to drive us over to Burgessville, son," he said. "What say you and I go over there and bring the old Bearcat home?"

Back in his own home that night, Inspector Tearle relived his greatest case when, at long last, he was able to tell his parents all about it. He even did the Swami's Card Box trick for them — complete with turban this time — and this time Thumbs, who had been invited to stay for dinner, managed to hold onto the torn corner of the card. When Roger removed the dome of the Swami's Card Box, a card lay on the tray that was complete except for one corner — and Thumbs' corner fitted it perfectly.

Roger's purpose in doing the trick was not mere entertainment in this instance, however. He wanted to explain what had finally put him on the right track.

"All of a sudden it came to me," he said. "I know I shouldn't tell anything about how we magicians do our tricks, but part of the trick here is that I plant a corner from a different card among the torn-up pieces — a corner that fits another card. Suddenly,

when I was yelling at Shirley for finding another corner, I started to say, 'It's not the same card!' And
right then — "

"I get it!" cried Thumbs. "Right then you must
have thought, 'And it's not the same *car*, either!' "

"Right!" said Roger, gazing approvingly at his
friend. "The words were even so close, car and card,
that I think that helped."

Mr. Tearle sat back from the table and waggled
his head as he favored his son with a long and
thoughtful look.

"And for nearly twenty-four hours, while a state-
wide hunt was going on for him, you had that boy
tucked away up there in your tree house!" he said.

"Roger, I can't wait for you to grow up and get married and move away. I don't think I can stand much more of this."

"I didn't put him there, Dad," Roger pointed out. "I *found* him there."

"Yes, I know. But — but — well, anyway, it all worked out fine, I must admit. Good grief, Milford won't be able to do enough for Hazy now. He'll probably give him everything you can think of, and even spend some time with him for a change."

"Sure," said Roger, "until he gets too busy again."

His father looked surprised by this comment. But then, after a moment's reflection, he nodded.

"Well, yes. I know what you mean. Milford's a big-time operator, with lots of important interests."

"Sure he is," said Roger. He gazed across the table at his father. "You know how I feel when I look at Mr. Milford?"

"No, how?"

He stared down at the Swami's Card Box, suddenly shy, then gave his father a quick, embarrassed grin.

"Lucky," said Roger.